last refuge

A Thomas Family Novel

Kristi Cramer

Amazon ASIN: B0BDXNKMT8

Amazon Paperback ISBN: 978-0-9862105-8-7

Editor: Monica Black, Word Nerd Editing

Cover Designer: 100 Covers

www.kristicramerbooks.com

contents

Syracuse, Kansas, is a real town. However, the people and places in this book—and all of the planned Thomas Family Novels—are totally fictitious. I have taken liberties with everything from the history to the agriculture to the businesses and bus stop downtown. I'm sure the real Syracuse has history and drama of its own, and while the tale I spin in these pages could happen there, Last Refuge is pure fiction. So enjoy. If you happen to pass through Syracuse, have a look around, stop for a meal, and help support a fine American town. Just don't expect it to resemble my fictional version.

Also of note, Last Refuge introduces a new character who speaks Louisiana Creole, which is considered an Endangered Language as fewer than ten thousand people in the world speak it. The words are similar to French and Cajun, but Louisiana Creole is a distinct language which has unique spelling that looks more phonetic than its parent language. See the Author's Note at the end for more information about Louisiana Creole.

chapter
one

Savannah Montault De Saint-Cirié breathed a sigh of relief as she saw hints of a town ahead. After hours of open road and endless, low-rolling hills of Kansas prairie, she'd begun to wonder if she had finally reached the end of the world.

Squinting, she read the road sign through the heat haze emanating from the pavement.

Syracuse – 5 miles

She'd been fighting highway hypnosis for the last hundred miles, and now with signs of life ahead, she shook it off. It was long minutes before the cluster of buildings began to take individual shape on the horizon. She kicked off the cruise control when she spotted the truck stop up ahead.

Visions of a fresh pot of coffee danced in her head like the late summer mirages rising from the road.

It was getting late and stopping for the night was appealing. She dreaded the thought of sleeping in her car again, but could she afford to actually lay down in a bed for a change? She hadn't splurged on a room in more than a week, as her cash supply dwindled with no prospects of refreshing it.

Something had to give. Did she dare ask for directions to a cheap motel?

One thing was certain: caffeine was necessary before she could come to any decisions. She pulled in at the Chew, Brew & Pit Crew truck stop and parked in front of the café. Turning the engine off, she sat for a moment, still feeling the vibrations of the road under her hands. Eventually she grabbed her purse, opened the door of her 1980 Chevy Citation, and put both feet on the ground.

Heat rolled against her in waves. A thick tang of old motor oil and spilled fuel clawed at her throat, making her hurry to lock her car and head inside. At least there was no humidity to frizz the natural curls of her hair.

Once inside the glass doors she scanned the customers, automatically checking for familiar faces even though she didn't really expect she'd see Laurencett. She knew in her heart the agent wouldn't come for her personally, and she would never see it coming when. . . *if* he found her.

Spotting the sign for the restroom, she made her way across the dining area and pushed through the door, automatically checking out shoes under the stall doors. Only one of the three stalls was occupied. The old, dirty cowboy boots weren't cause for alarm, and she breathed a little easier.

Minutes later, she washed her hands then ran a wet brush through her hair, trying to tame the unruly mass. It wasn't a total wreck, but there wasn't much to be done until she could shower. With a quick twist, she pulled her thick hair off her shoulders and tied it into a knot at the base of her neck.

As she checked her teeth before refreshing her lipstick, the door opened behind her and she jumped, almost dropping the tube. The woman who entered, friendly-faced and in her sixties, smiled at her before disappearing into a vacant stall. A long moment passed before Savannah stopped shaking enough to continue.

Back in the café, she chose a seat at the far end of the counter, twisting the stool so she could see the door.

A cheerful blonde walked up with a coffee pot and flipped the nearest mug right-side-up before pouring the richly scented liquid. Savannah felt life returning just at the smell.

"You're a lifesaver," she told the girl, taking note of her name badge. "Thank you, Kylie."

"You looked like you could use a cup," she said, placing a menu and a bundle of silverware wrapped in a napkin to the right of Savannah's hand. "You just holler when you're ready to order."

"*Mersi*," she said, then bit her lips closed.

The girl did a double take. "My boss speaks French too," she said after a moment, then moved on to fill some more mugs, but Savannah couldn't hear any more words over the ringing in her ears. The fact that this girl's boss spoke French—*she'd said French, not Louisiana Creole*—was absurd, but it didn't stop the fear that switched on like a light in her mind.

It took several moments of deep breathing before she dared to lift the mug to her lips, fearing her hands would shake and the hot liquid would spill out and burn her. At last she got herself under control and took a sip. The bold roast was such a balm to her soul, Savannah easily kept herself from reacting when the woman from the restroom sat down beside her.

"What can I get for you, Grandma?" Kylie asked, stepping up behind the counter.

"A new cook," the woman said with a sigh. "I'm getting run ragged out at the ranch."

Savannah tried, but she couldn't help eavesdropping.

"No word back from Esmeralda?"

"Nothing good, I'm afraid. Her mother is very ill but still hanging on, bless her heart. She said her father is taking it very hard. She's not sure how long he'll last if her mother passes."

"Aw, that's sad news." Kylie wiped the counter with a damp rag in contemplation. Whomever this Esmeralda was, it was apparent she was dear to both women. "I could check with Dylan and see if he can spare me to come out a couple days a week."

Savannah watched as the older woman gazed around the busy café. "It's still high tourist season. I can hardly deprive Dylan of his best waitress."

"He'd understand," Kylie said, resting her hand on the woman's and giving it a squeeze.

A voice called for coffee from the other side of the diner, and the girl lifted her hand in acknowledgement. "I'll be right back."

"I can cook." Savannah didn't know what came over her to say that out loud. "I'm sorry," she said quickly. "I'm road weary, I didn't mean to listen in."

The woman looked at her in a way that made Savannah's insides tremble. Not with fear, but from an understanding that this woman could read her like an open book. "You're not from around here." It wasn't a question, neither was it a challenge. It was merely a statement of fact.

Savannah shook her head, sorry she'd spoken at all. The thick accent even she knew was unusual had given her away. She'd been working on concealing it under a Midwestern twang. With little success, apparently.

"I'm just passing through." When the woman cocked her head, she felt obliged to explain why she'd mentioned that she could cook. "See, I'm in no hurry. . . and frankly, I could use some money."

The woman nodded as though everything now made sense. "I'm Maddy. Maddy Thomas," she said, holding out her hand.

Savannah took it to receive a firm shake and answered automatically, forgetting everything in one reckless moment. "Savannah Saint . . . ." She swallowed, but it was too late to take it back. "Saint-Aime."

The woman's expression told her she'd taken note of the hesitation, but she didn't pursue it. "Esmeralda, our cook, went to Mexico to be with her mother. We've been without help for three months." After another measured look, she continued. "The Lazy J Ranch is about thirty minutes outside of town, and I'll be honest, there's not many folks who want to take on cooking and laundry for eight ranch hands plus two farm hands most days. My husband and I usually take care of ourselves, but I've been doing most all of it since she left. I found a high school kid who comes out to do dishes, and I get a little help in my garden from the farm hands, but I'm not as young as I used to be." She spread her hands in a helpless gesture.

Despite her own situation, Savannah felt herself getting caught up in the woman's story and silently assessed whether this was something she could or should look further into. She could cook, yes, but for ten strangers? And she didn't know what the laundry situation would be like for that many people. It would be a lot of work. But. . . this little town was certainly off the beaten path. If she could crawl into a backwater hole and disappear, she might feel safe for the first time in too long to consider.

She realized she was staring at the woman when Maddy laid a hand on her arm. "Are you all right, dear?"

"*Wi*. I mean, yes. I was just considering. . . that is. . . maybe I'm in a way to help you out." She stopped, inwardly cursing the lack of focus that was surely going to get herself killed. Her attempt at a Midwestern accent was utterly failing. Not only was her thick "*Nawlins*" drawl showing, so were her Creole roots . . . .

Time for something different. She leaned close. "You see, I'm thinking we could help each other."

"Oh?"

Maddy's gaze searched hers, and Savannah tried her best to look earnest. Then she laid it on thick, though it went against her every instinct to *embellish* the truth.

"I wouldn't tell my story to just anyone, Maddy, but I'm desperate. *Mo bezon*. . . I need to get lost, and a job thirty minutes outside a small town may just be enough."

Maddy's eyes widened in surprise as Kylie returned to freshen up their coffee mugs. "Have you decided what you want?" Kylie asked as she poured, not looking up.

Savannah held Maddy's gaze for a moment longer, then picked up the menu and glanced at it. She couldn't afford much. "Just a cup of the soup of the day will do," she said, remembering to smile at the girl.

"A cup? Not a bowl?"

"A cup, yeah." She returned the menu in an attempt to head off more questions from the girl. When Kylie took the order to the window, she turned to find Maddy still watching her.

"I take it you're in some kind of trouble?"

Savannah couldn't tell by the tone of her voice if Maddy was buying it or not, but she had at least taken the bait, so she dialed it up a notch. "You could say that."

She picked up her napkin bundle and stripped off the

paper band holding the silverware together, then began folding it over upon itself as she looked again at Maddy.

"I'm down to my last few dollars and running out of road. If I don't find something soon, I'll have to use my debit card, and my *husband*—" she choked out the word, ". . . will find me."

She let herself begin to shake at the thought, knowing the emotion would help cover the lie of who Laurencett was to her. *Not my husband, just the man who wants to drag me back to hell.*

Maddy's gaze turned soft with understanding. "Oh, my dear," she breathed, reaching again to place her hand on Savannah's arm.

Drawing a shuddering breath, she let the woman comfort her for a moment, until Kylie came back with the cup of soup. The girl looked between the two of them, and Savannah saw the questions in her eyes.

"Sa—" Maddy began, but Savannah grasped her hand and squeezed.

"Please, call me Dawn. I shouldn't have given you my real name."

Maddy nodded in understanding, then continued. "Dawn, I would love it if you would follow me out to the ranch tonight. We can talk more out there and see if you really want to take on the job of feeding us out at the Lazy J."

"You cook?" Kylie said in surprise. "And you want to cook for my grandma?"

"Kylie!" Maddy sounded surprised at her granddaughter's questioning tone.

"No. I mean, it's cool. It's just. . . you're so beautiful. I wouldn't expect someone with such beauty would be willing to slop food around for a bunch of dirty cowboys." Kylie held up her hand as Maddy appeared ready to protest again. "I mean dirt dirty, Grandma. You know I love one of those dirty cowboys."

Maddy shook her head at her granddaughter, but Savannah could tell it was good-natured exasperation. "One could very well say you're too beautiful to work in a diner, dear."

To Savannah's amusement, Kylie blushed. She spoke up quickly to spare the child any more discomfort. "It's all right. I take it as a compliment, but I do need a job."

"Finish your soup, dear, and we'll talk some more," Maddy said.

chapter
two

Colton Thomas the Third—Trip to his family and friends—felt major relief that the day was almost over as he rode toward the barn. It had been one of the more challenging days he'd had in a while.

The new hand was supposed to have been experienced, which was why he'd been sent out to tend the cattle in the yearling herd. But instead of moving them to the correct pasture, he'd set them loose into a neighbor's sorghum field —and nobody had caught the mistake until the neighbor showed up to complain. They'd spent the better part of the afternoon rounding up fifty head, then re-stringing the fence line the rookie had taken down, all while Adam Braxton howled about the damage and demanded restitution.

The man had had every reason to howl. The cattle had done considerable damage to a crop rapidly becoming lucrative as a gluten-free grain. And that had only made Trip feel worse. He wanted to be angry at Braxton, but it was a Lazy J hand who had been in the wrong. And Trip had been the one to hire Ned Callow to replace Kenny and put him on the yearlings. The only one he could truly be mad at was himself.

Ned rode a few paces behind him, quiet enough to be walking his horse on proverbial eggshells. Trip hadn't been able to say a word to the boy for fear he'd unleash the anger he felt at himself and direct it toward the kid.

As the sun set behind them, casting their shadows long across the ground and turning the eastern sky to the deep reds and purples of twilight, Trip tried to pull himself together. He'd like to put the whole day behind him, but he still had to tell his father about the incident.

When they crested the hill and headed down into the hollow where the ranch buildings lay in the glooming dusk, he heaved a big sigh.

Ned cleared his throat. "You want I should report to Mr. Thomas and tell him what I done?"

"No, Ned. Ultimately, I'm responsible. You go on in and wash up for supper—after you take care of Rocket."

The big bay Nokota gelding flicked his ears forward upon hearing his name. He and Scotchie exchanged whinnies, as though having their own conversation. That finally brought a smile to Trip's face.

Inside the barn, Trip took his time brushing Scotchie, even currying the burrs out of his tail. Unable to delay the inevitable forever, he left Scotchie's stall after a full half hour and headed for the house. What he wanted was a good meal, a cold beer, an easy confession to his father, and a good night's sleep so he could have a better day tomorrow.

When he stepped out of the barn, something was different, though it took a moment for it to register. There was a new car parked behind Momma's VW bug. Well, "new" was. . . optimistic. The squat, ugly pillbug of a car was quite possibly older than he was, but Trip didn't recognize it.

Crossing the yard, he took the porch steps in two bounds, whipped through the screen door, and toed off his boots. He tossed his hat at the rack, where it balanced on the hook next to his father's then fell to the floor as he headed upstairs to clean up.

A stranger's voice coming from the kitchen gave him pause. It was a woman's voice, low and throaty, with an accent Trip couldn't readily identify. Something Southern, but stronger or. . . different. Tempted as he was to listen in, he either needed to step into the kitchen to identify himself and say hello or come back down showered and ready to face his father with the bad news.

He opted for the shower. Maybe by the time he came back downstairs the stranger would be gone, and Trip could get chewed out in private.

Once upstairs, his hopes for that were dashed when he saw the door to the guest room standing open and a suitcase—a gym bag, really—sitting on the foot of the bed. The stranger was going to stay the night.

With a groan, Trip hurried through the process of showering and changed into some fresh clothes before heading back downstairs.

The stranger was talking again as he rounded the corner, and he stopped stock still at the sight of her.

". . . it was just the sort of thing you might expect," she was saying. "I gave him everything, and—" Catching sight of him, she broke off. "Hello."

He shouldn't be staring, but the woman was breathtaking. She was short and curvaceous, her form-fitting skirt and blouse combo totally out of place in his mother's kitchen. Her hair—long, black, and curly—was pulled back from her face into a bun at the base of her neck, revealing a face deserving of a Michelangelo sculpture. Light brown skin with warm undertones graced cheekbones that accented her round face, and her slightly flattened nose perfectly complimented her full lips.

What really stopped him in his tracks were her eyes. Thick lashes slanted over eyes of emerald-green, immediately conjuring visions of a dimly lit bedroom and two bodies engaged in activities he . . . .

Momma would take a switch to his hide if she knew what he was thinking. And since his momma had always been able to tell what was on his mind, he knew without even looking at her he had better shape his act up. He recalled his manners about the time Momma cleared her throat.

"Hello." He continued into the room, approaching her. She didn't extend her hand, so he didn't try for a handshake. "I'm Trip," he said. "Colton Thomas the Third."

"Ah yes," she said, "Maddy's eldest son." The woman smiled, though she still didn't attempt to shake hands with him. "My name is Sa . . . ," she hesitated and glanced at Momma, "Savannah Saint-Aime. But please, call me Dawn."

Trip raised his eyebrows but nodded. "Pleasure to meet you, Miss Dawn."

"Dawn has agreed to cook for us," Momma said with evident pleasure. "She helped me with the meal for the hands in the chow hall as well as here at the house. I think you'll agree she has the skill, we just have to hope she'll have the forbearance to stay."

Before Trip could respond, Daddy came through from the master suite at the back of the house. He was showered, shaved, and appeared to have his mind set on supper.

"Miss Dawn," Daddy said, out of habit tipping the hat he no longer wore.

"Mr. Thomas," the woman said, dipping her head.

Trip decided the name Dawn didn't fit her, unless the two names were together. Savannah was much more suited to her elegant clothes, her beauty, her laugh. But Dawn suited the way she stole the light from a room just so it could focus on her.

He gave his head a small shake to dislodge the poetry.

"Let's go to the dining room, shall we?" Momma said. All three gestured for Dawn to go first. She laughed a comfortable, easy-going chuckle as she picked up a covered dish and crossed into the next room. Momma lifted the bun warmer and followed, leaving Daddy to carry the soup tureen. Trip grabbed the bamboo tray that held the serving utensils.

Daddy took his usual seat at the head of the table, and Momma sat beside him, giving their guest the seat of honor across the table from Daddy. Trip hurried to adjust Dawn's chair for her, then sat down across from Momma. As was their custom, Momma and Daddy joined hands. Trip linked with his father in the same way, then watched his mother for cues of whether to include their guest. When Momma rested her free hand on the table palm up, Trip followed suit.

"Would you care to join us in saying grace for this meal?" Trip marveled at the way Momma could ask the question without putting any pressure or guilt out there.

Savannah hesitantly put her hands in theirs, and Trip closed his fingers lightly around her cool, dry fingers. There was a kind of electricity that leapt from her skin to his. He nearly flinched from the power of it, and never heard the prayer his mother invoked over the meal.

When she slid her fingers away from his, he reached for the bun warmer with forced calm and lifted the metal lid, automatically offering her first selection of the contents, which turned out to be biscuits. She smiled at him as she lifted one out, and he felt himself blushing as he smiled back.

Good grief. He needed to get ahold of himself. *Obviously I need to get out more. I don't even know how to behave around a beautiful woman.* Not that Jules wasn't beautiful, but his relationship with Jules wasn't what he considered traditional.

"So," Daddy started, passing him the covered dish, which turned out to be broiled sirloin steaks, "anything you need to tell me about, son?"

Trip snapped his attention back to his father and cleared his throat. By his tone, Daddy already knew about the Braxton disaster. He couldn't try to evade it. Not that he would have.

"Yes, sir. I put Ned on the yearlings and told him to let them into the south pasture. I assumed he knew where I meant since it was one of the first places I took him when he started. I should have checked up on him, but…well, the upshot is he turned them out into Braxton's sorghum, and they did a fair bit of damage before we got 'em sorted back onto our land. It was my fault. I take the blame."

Daddy grunted as he took the ladle from Momma and looked into the soup tureen. The soup he ladled into his bowl was like no soup Trip had seen before. It was a cream base with orange chunks and green flecks floating in it. Trip and his father both frowned, but Daddy was apparently too hungry to question what it was.

"Braxton will try to jack up the cost of the damage," Daddy said. "I expect it'll be your responsibility to know the true extent and get a third-party estimate if needed."

"Yes, sir," Trip said, holding back a sigh, both relieved and irritated. On the one hand, he was glad there wasn't a bigger stink about it. On the other, the last thing he wanted to do was deal with a neighbor like Braxton. The man always seemed to be looking for ways to get something more than his fair share out of what amounted to an accident.

Daddy passed him the soup tureen, and Trip looked inside the white ceramic pot with skepticism. He had to admit, the smell was heavenly. He lifted his gaze to Momma, who smiled.

"The soup is Dawn's."

He turned his head to their guest. "What's in it?"

"Spinach and sweet potato soup." She flashed him a decidedly secretive smile. "A family recipe. Be brave. Try it."

He bristled slightly at her insinuation he was too chicken to try the soup. It was just soup.

"Sure smells good," he said, and ladled his bowl almost to the rim. He would eat it all, just because she'd all but dared him.

SAVANNAH PLACED her biscuit in the bottom of her soup bowl. Trip offered the ladle, and she held the bowl out for him to serve her. She thanked him and pulled it away after only one scoop.

He gave a small frown. His gaze flicked to her plate, as if to question why she was taking such a small amount of food. That reaction was a pleasant change from the judgement she was used to: people telling her she ate too much. But it was too late now to ask for more on her first round. She would have seconds later. If she was still hungry.

Truth was, she hadn't been eating very well—hadn't had the money to—for a few weeks now, and she wasn't sure her stomach would allow her to ingest much.

Everyone at the table was watching her, and she realized they were waiting for her to take the first bite—another honor she was not used to. Feeling shy, she smiled down at her bowl, dipped her spoon into the soup, and put it to her lips, sipping up the savory liquid.

That was all Mr. Thomas needed. He began to eat with almost alarming speed. Mrs. Thomas had warned her he wasn't one to fuss over his food, but she hadn't realized that meant he would inhale it without even tasting.

The son appeared to be a little more discerning. He'd risen to the bait when she'd teased him about her soup, but he hadn't yet tried it. He attacked his steak with only a little less ferocity than his father.

A glance at Maddy told her this was normal for the men. Maddy gave her an encouraging smile as she took a spoonful of soup.

"This is very good, Dawn."

"Thank you." She cut herself a tiny piece of steak, using her best table manners. When in doubt, her mother had always taught her perfect manners never go amiss.

"You didn't make that for the fellas outside, did you?" Trip dabbed at his lips with a napkin almost as an afterthought. He was on his second steak.

"No," she said. "Mrs. Thomas assured me it would be wasted effort. That, and we didn't have enough ingredients to serve so many."

Trip eyed the very large tureen that had been nearly full before they'd started. "If you say so."

His doubtful tone triggered the defense mechanism that had been drilled into her since she'd hit puberty: defend and deflect with flirty sass. "Oh, I do say so. If you try it, I think you'll like it very much. One bowl won't be enough."

He lifted an eyebrow at her, rising to the challenge

again. She noted his wide blue eyes and finely sculpted lips and cheekbones, trying to determine if the mind was as sharp as the looks were handsome. Her cheeks warmed, and she turned her thoughts away from a learned behavior that had never really sat well with her. He wasn't a prospect she'd been charged to acquire—and she wasn't here to look at fine men.

Trip dipped up a spoonful of the soup and looked at her as he raised it to his lips. She watched with interest, half-hoping he'd fall out of his chair in surprise.

Once he tasted it, his gaze dropped to the bowl, and a bemused expression crossed his face. "It *is* good. What's in it?"

It was her turn to raise an eyebrow. "Spinach, sweet potatoes, and sausage," she said slyly. She wasn't about to list every ingredient, from the celery, onions, bell peppers, and garlic to the heavy cream and subtle spices. "Above that, it's a secret family recipe."

"She wouldn't even let me watch," Maddy said with cheerful mock resentment.

Mr. Thomas served himself his third bowlful. She was gratified he had finally slowed after the first two and now seemed to be savoring the taste.

Trip ate more of the soup, his steak forgotten, and Savannah smiled. The dish had been the result of a search through Mrs. Thomas's cupboard and refrigerator. She'd only had to make a couple small adjustments and was pleased it had turned out.

chapter
three

Supper was over. The men had retired to talk business in the den while Savannah helped clear the table and do the dishes. As when they were cooking, she found Maddy a pleasure to work with. They moved around each other with ease, Maddy drying while Savannah washed. They had cleaned the kitchen as they'd cooked, so there was only the table and service dishes, and the task went by swiftly.

They worked in near silence, although Savannah could tell it was in part because Maddy was waiting for her to speak, to tell her story. She had begun to earlier, while they'd been waiting for the men to show up, and Maddy was waiting for more.

"Do you think I should go out and check on the dishes in the. . . what did you call it? Chow hall? It won't be good to have them sit overnight."

Maddy waved a dismissive hand. "Carson will get them. You and I need to plan for tomorrow's breakfast."

"Oh. All right." She passed over a rinsed plate, and Maddy accepted it.

"I've been keeping it simple these days, lots of oatmeal

and scrambled eggs, that sort of thing, but they've been wanting more variety. Esmeralda had them pretty spoiled with sausage and bacon and biscuits and gravy and eggs— a whole mess of options I frankly don't have the time to clean up after. Maybe you know how it is?"

Savannah nodded. "It's not so much the cooking as the cleaning up after a bunch of men, yes?"

"Exactly. Esmeralda had her son to help her, and I'll keep looking for some consistent help for you. Carson only comes out after the evening meal. He babysits his siblings during the day, so you'll be on your own for breakfast and lunch. I don't know if we'll be able to keep him once school starts next week."

Savannah nodded, as if it mattered. She was confident she could do the cleanup. It was cooking a timely meal for so many that had her the most concerned. Maddy had made it look easy tonight, but she was under no illusions her first attempts would be less than stellar. She had no idea whether she could live up to the challenge, it was just a matter of doing.

The thought triggered a memory. A dark face, eyes wide, mouth forming a tiny "o" of fear. A woman's voice. "You never know what you are capable of until it comes down to the wire. Then it's just a matter of doing what needs to be done."

"Dawn?" Maddy said, and Savannah realized her false name had been called several times.

"Sorry, I was a thousand miles away."

Maddy gave her a sad smile. "I know you don't know me, Savannah, but I hope you discover you can trust me."

"Trust is hard for me these days," Savannah said, not missing the fact that Maddy had used her real name. "I'm sure you can imagine. My. . . husband has connections all over the country. The thought of him finding me is terrifying." She held onto the counter so tight, her knuckles turned white from the strain. When she realized it, she let loose slowly.

Maddy read her fear, again missing the lie, and put a comforting hand on her back. "I put your bag in the guest room upstairs. Tomorrow we'll see about getting you settled into the cook's quarters."

"Thanks so much once again for this opportunity, Mrs. Thomas. You don't know. . . you have no idea how much this means to me . . . ."

Maddy enfolded her in a hug, and for a moment Savannah let herself dream this was the solution to all her problems. A job in a place so small it was hardly a blip on a map, well off the beaten path, working for a woman who was the soul of kindness.

Yes, for that moment, she felt she could make this place a home.

Then she remembered: home is not always safe. Everyone she had ever trusted had either failed her or proved to have less than her best interests in mind. Everyone. The only person she could rely on was herself. Best to keep her eye on that cold, hard fact.

UPSTAIRS, Savannah stood at the foot of the bed and stared down at her bag. All her clothes were soiled—worn too many days in a row. The cleanest item was her pajamas, and that was only because she'd slept in her car most nights. She was dying to be clean and wondered if Maddy's hospitality included use of the bathroom long enough to shower.

As if in answer, she turned at a sound in the hall and found Maddy there, holding a folded towel and washcloth.

"The bathroom is across the hall, dear. Help yourself. You're welcome to join me downstairs after, but our day starts an hour before sunrise, and that means five AM, so you'll probably want to turn in."

"Yes, I am tired." She had driven over five hundred miles before stopping in Syracuse, then helped prepare two meals. She was exhausted.

"I'll wake you in the morning, then. Goodnight, Sava. . . Dawn."

Savannah opened her mouth to tell her it was okay to call her Savannah, but she held back. In her bones, she felt she could trust Maddy Thomas, but what about the others on the ranch? What happened when one of them heard Maddy call her by her real name and mentioned it in town?

"Goodnight, Mrs. Thomas."

The gentle woman smiled kindly, then tapped the door-frame once before she turned to leave.

Savannah waited until she heard the woman's footsteps on the stairs before she crossed the hall and entered the bathroom, carrying the towel and her small bag of bathroom sundries.

The room was simple, white, clean, with a pale blue shower curtain surrounding an ancient clawfoot tub. A tiny window was open to catch the evening breeze that stirred the curtain, and chirring of cicadas carried through the screen.

She bent to turn on the water and let it run while she peeled out of her clothes. Looking in the mirror while she undressed, she didn't see herself. She saw a face several shades darker than her own, gaze locked onto her as the voice pleaded for mercy.

Shaking her head sharply, she kicked her dirty clothes against the door and turned to feel the water, adjusting the knobs to get the perfect temperature. When she stepped into the clawfoot tub, she sighed as the water and steam enveloped her. As much as she didn't really feel she deserved it, this was a special kind of heaven, however short term it was to luxuriate under the stream.

TRIP DIDN'T HAVE the energy for his usual bounding pace up the stairs to his bedroom. His session with his father had been grueling, with Daddy going over everything he knew about the current prices on sorghum crops and his insistence that Trip write down everything he could recall from the incident—both his own memories and what Ned had told him.

Now all he could think about was his bed and getting as much sleep as possible in the mere seven hours he had before sunup.

Just as he passed the bathroom, the door opened upon Savannah—Dawn, he corrected himself—wrapped in a terry cloth towel that did a thoroughly inadequate job of covering her curvaceous body. He looked up quickly, but the way the white towel contrasted against the warm brown tones of her skin etched into his mind. Her wet hair hung in thick waves over her shoulder to her ample bustline. He had to drag his eyes northward again.

"Excuse me, Miss Dawn," he said. "I was just headed to my room." He gestured vaguely toward the door to the room next to hers. "I didn't mean to get in your way."

"Nonsense," she protested. "If anything, I'm in your way. I didn't expect to see you and left my nightshirt in there." She pointed to the guest room, and he did indeed see a golden lump of fabric on the bed next to the bag.

His gaze was drawn back to her face, and he caught himself studying her rather too intently for a hallway encounter. Before he could stop himself, he opened his mouth and said, "Where're you from, Miss Dawn? If you don't mind me asking."

The question was blunt, and he was rather mortified he'd just up and asked it. He was about to take it back when she put a hand up to his shoulder. She held his gaze, and he swore he saw a flash of fear in her eyes, then she said something in a low voice that almost reminded him of the French he'd learned in high school.

"I'm sorry," he said, tilting his head to the side, "I didn't catch that. Was that French?"

It seemed to be a test of some kind, because she smiled with something that looked like relief and dropped her hand. "I should tell you I'm from some little village in the French Pyrenees."

"But you're not?" He was getting confused, and her standing there wearing only a towel was an unfair distraction.

"Or maybe I'm from Quebec, yes?" She said it like "kay-beck."

He shook his head, trying to focus, and she laughed.

"Perhaps I'm really from New Orleans." She said it like "Nawlins," and it took him a moment to recognize where she was talking about. She put her finger to her lips. "It will be our little secret, yes?"

"Which one?" he asked, annoyed she seemed to be playing a pointless little game with him. "If you don't want to say, just tell me so."

Her expression told him she felt contrite. "Truly, I'm from New Orleans, and the language is Louisiana Creole.

But if anyone else asks me to confirm this, I will deny and say I am *Quebequois*."

Trip blinked at her. "Why?"

She raised one eyebrow. "Perhaps I'm a spy, and if I tell you, I must kill you, *non*?" She winked. "I make bad jokes." As quickly as she'd teased him, she became serious. "There's a man looking for me. If he finds me, bad things will happen. This is why I ask you to keep my secret, *shær*."

While he stood still, trying to figure out what to believe, Savannah stepped up to him and tiptoed to press a butterfly kiss on his cheek. Then she was gone, shutting the door to the guest room with a quiet click.

"What the heck?" he asked out loud. She had fired so many stories at him, he had no idea what to believe. Her flirty manner had disconcerted him as much as the disparate stories, not to mention her state of undress. "I think I had better keep my distance from this one," he muttered under his breath.

It should be easy. She would surely be moving into the cook's house tomorrow, and he wouldn't have to see her very often at all. But something about her sultry voice and sinful curves, combined with a vulnerability he may well have imagined, guaranteed he would be thinking about her for a long while.

So much for getting a good night's sleep.

Shær. Her voice whispered in his mind, and he thought he recognized the word as a French endearment. *Keep my secret.*

But which story was truly her secret? He'd have to find out what she'd told his mother in the morning.

SAVANNAH LEANED against the door after she shut it, her heart racing. What had she just done?

She'd intended to dazzle the cowboy with a brilliant lie, using the flirty attitude that had been ingrained in her since puberty, but something had incited her to share her truth. Trip's eyes, his open and honest expression, the way he gallantly fought his physical attraction to her. . . all had softened her approach. She doubted he realized part of the things she said were indeed the truth, but still, it was foolish of her to give even a hint of her origins to anyone this far away from home.

It was the risk she'd taken, choosing to run so far west. As long as she stayed in the South, especially the south-eastern states, her distinctive New Orleans drawl was not so out of the ordinary. But out here on the western plains, her accent and thoughtless slips into Creole stood out and drew attention—potentially dangerous attention.

Staying close to home had seemed like a poor option when she'd left. There were too many ways she could be found. Traffic cameras and security cameras in every store and public building she entered. She hadn't been able to breathe.

This place in Kansas was the first time she'd spoken to anyone without feeling tied into some greater world of surveillance and observation, and it had affected her ability to stay on track, keep her story straight.

In time, she heard another door shut in the hall and knew Trip had gone to his room. She stepped away from the door and crossed to the bed. With quick motions, she slipped her gold satin nightie on and let the towel drop, catching it with her foot and lifting it to her hand so she could drape it over the back of the chair in front of a small desk. She moved her bag over to the chair, then turned down the sheets, crawled into bed, and reached to turn off the lamp.

As darkness enfolded her, she took note of the soft mattress. The sheets and duvet were just the right thickness to comfort her on a warm summer evening without over-heating. The pillow was perfect for lying on her side. She snuggled, back to the door, and tried to sleep.

She was so exhausted, her eyes wouldn't stay open even if she'd used toothpicks. Sleep claimed her . . . .

Until the vision came back. Dion's face. Accusing now.

"Savannah," the woman's voice called in a sing-song parody of a loving parent. "Savannah. This death is on you. It could have been avoided if you'd only obeyed."

She sat up in a sweat, surprised to hear another light knock on the door.

"Dawn, it's time to get up."

chapter
four

It was still dark outside when Trip gave up on trying to sleep.

He'd never realized the wall his room shared with the guest room was so thin. Savannah Dawn's every movement sounded as though she'd tossed and turned beside him all night, and he couldn't get the vision of her towel-wrapped body out of his mind.

Finally, he threw back the sheet and sat up on the edge of the bed. He scrubbed his hands over his eyes, his elbows on his knees.

"For crying out loud," he said at last, his voice low to keep it from carrying.

Moving as silently as possible in the old house, he slipped on his jeans, grabbed a shirt and some fresh socks out of a drawer, and stole barefoot down the stairs in the dark. By the yard lights shining through the front window, he put on his shirt and tucked it in, then hopped on one foot while he pulled on his socks and boots. He settled his Stetson on his head and opened the door.

Outside, the fresh morning air was brisk with the first hint of fall, and he reached back in to grab his jean jacket before making his way to the barn. He inhaled deeply and said a little prayer of gratitude that this was his life. Even after a crummy day like yesterday, he wouldn't dream of doing anything else.

When he entered the barn and approached Scotchie's stall on the close end of the stable bay, his gelding whickered a soft greeting.

"Hey, boy. You care if I wake you early?" he asked, though it wasn't unusual for him to come out before daylight.

Scotchie snorted and tossed his head, earning a few answering noises from the other stalls.

"Shhh, you big clod. Don't stir everyone up. You'll get Deke down here with his rifle, wondering what's going on."

It was pretty much impossible to saddle a horse without making any noise, but over the years, Trip had gotten pretty good at being quiet enough not to wake anyone in the bunkhouses. Before long he was on his way out the stable aisle, past the hulking shadows of machinery in the main enclosure on the way to the big barn doors, trailed by a saddled and eager Scotchie.

By the way the air tasted, dawn was still an hour or so off, so he closed the big barn door behind him, then the gate to the pasture once they'd gone through. The gate squealed a bit when he shut it, and he made a mental note to oil the hinges when he got back.

Deke was a light sleeper, so he lifted a hand toward the foreman's cottage on the off chance he had roused the man, then guided Scotchie to the left. Once outside the circles of light from the yard, he gave the gelding his head so the horse could choose his path in the ink-black landscape. Scotchie knew the drill and made his way to the slope leading up to the western rim of the hollow where the Home Place lay nestled, sheltered from the prairie winds.

It was second nature to trust the big horse, and he could predict almost to the step when he would feel Scotchie begin to climb the slope. Leaning his head back to look up at an indigo canvas filled with jeweled points of brilliance, Trip breathed in the early morning air, allowing it to scrub the cobwebs from his mind.

Once they reached the crest, Scotchie paused and automatically turned to the east, as they so often did. Reaching out, Trip slapped the gelding's neck affectionately. "We're pretty early today," he said. "Sun won't be up for at least half an hour. Let's ride out and check that repair."

With a nudge of his heel and a click of his tongue, Trip urged Scotchie to turn back around, and they walked across the prairie. They could have made better time but the moon was down, making the countryside pitch black, and it wasn't like they were in any hurry.

They'd walked about a quarter mile when Trip became aware of the landscape around him forming out of the darkness. He looked up to see the stars winking out one by one as the night began to fade. Not long after, the first rays of light shot out across the land, lighting the low hills in the west. He and Scotchie turned to face the east, where the sky glowed golden yellow with the approaching sun.

As they watched, the light burst forward, dazzling his eyes until he closed them and let the sun's first rays bathe him with a gentle warmth.

Sunrise was his favorite time of day. It reminded him that life went on, despite whatever was going on in his mind. He'd discovered the heart-easing qualities of that quintessential time of day quite on accident, having had trouble sleeping after Kate rode off into the sunset. Even now, he could chase away her mocking laughter with a sunrise. Although today, there was a new thing—a new someone—between him and the old memory.

Instead of Kate's ginger locks and ice-blue eyes peering out at him from the window of the Greyhound bus, he saw emerald eyes twinkling with laughter and a seductive, saucy wink—eyes that gave him hope he'd finally be able to put Kate and his broken heart behind him.

Part of him took note of the sunrise illuminating a line of black-bellied clouds in the distance, burning them fiery red for a few telling moments.

"Gonna rain today."

Scotchie didn't so much as flick an ear in response, and Trip sighed. "Right. Let's check that fence then get back down for breakfast, shall we?"

That had one ear swiveling back toward him, and he laughed. Trust food to be the motivator for his greedy horse.

SAVANNAH WIPED her arm across her brow as she glanced at the clock. It was already after eleven, and she still had to prepare lunch for the men who would be coming back to the chow hall for the noon meal.

Breakfast had gone well, with Maddy's help, but the kitchen attached to the chow hall had been in such a state of neglect, she'd been hesitant to use it. The cooktop and one worktop were clean, and clean dishes were stacked on another counter, but it was chaotic. She would never say anything to disrespect Maddy, but it was apparent the woman had been having trouble keeping up.

After they'd brewed four gallons of coffee, whipped up

a huge double-burner pan of four dozen scrambled eggs on the gas stove, toasted two loaves of bread in the oven, and fried more strips of bacon than she'd cared to count, she'd been briefly introduced to the ranch hands.

The men had mumbled greetings and stared at her briefly, but mostly just tucked into the food in a pre-coffee daze before shambling out the door. She hadn't caught many names and resolved she would get better introductions at dinnertime, when everyone was more awake.

Then Maddy had gone back up to the main house, leaving her with a promise to return in the early afternoon to discuss dinner plans.

A quick inspection of the so-called clean dishes led to the discovery that Carson apparently suffered from the typical man's belief that dishes only needed to be washed on the inside. To get rid of the oily feel on the exteriors, Savannah decide every dish needed to be washed again before being put away.

That had taken her a good two hours, then she'd tackled the cooktop and oven, giving it a deep cleaning she was sure hadn't been undertaken in months. Then the countertops got scrubbed, including the central island surface. Finally, she swept and mopped the wide planks of the wooden floor.

She was tired, but it felt good to have done so much. It was more work than she'd ever done in her life, the sheer scale of it making her brief stint in a shared apartment in college—freedom she hadn't been allowed to maintain for long—look like child's play.

What she liked best was the way the work consumed her energy and concentration, leaving no room to dwell on the past or worry about the future. There was only the next thing to do to create a space she could work in.

Maddy had told her to be ready in case some of the

hands returned for lunch, but not to prepare anything unless and until someone showed up, so she took some time to familiarize herself with the food on hand, deciding she had enough lettuce, cheese, and ham to make sandwiches. She didn't know if anyone would want more coffee, but she knew she needed it, so she put a pot on, then looked around at what else needed to be done in her new domain.

On one side of the kitchen, a swinging door led to the chow hall. The trestle table, chairs, benches, and floors needed a good scrubbing—something she would tackle in the afternoon.

Several doors closed off a short hallway on the other side of the kitchen. A door on the left led to a utility room housing two industrial quality washers and dryers—and a rather disconcerting pile of laundry. A door on the right revealed a half-bathroom that would need blasting powder or hammer and chisel to clean. Beyond that, the door in the center led into a cozy cabin that gave the impression it hadn't been touched in a very long time.

Dust motes danced in the sunlight shining through the southern windows, but nothing else moved. The room was homey and comfortable, with a decidedly rustic feel. The walls were finished in rough-hewn paneling, the ceiling open and framed by beams of pine. A futon mattress with a native weave pattern settled upon a frame of split poles against one wall, behind a coffee table made from a slab of live-edge wood perched upon an artsy frame of antelope antlers. A bookshelf occupied one wall, and a flat-panel TV hung on the wall across from the futon, a haphazard jumble of game controllers in front of it. Simple decorations gave it a vague Southwestern flavor, reminding her that Esmeralda and her son—in whose home she now stood—were from Mexico.

Feeling a bit like an intruder, she crossed the room to a final door, which opened into a small bedroom suite. A wardrobe proved to contain women's clothing, and the double bed was made up with linen sheets, two big, fluffy pillows, and a woven comforter.

"Hello?" A voice from the kitchen interrupted her exploration.

With more than a touch of guilt, she exited the cabin and closed the door behind her, turning to see the younger Colton, Trip, standing in the doorway of the chow hall.

"Miss Dawn," he said, and swept his hat off his head. "I came to see how you were settling in and if you needed anything." She watched as his gaze took in the neat room. "You've already accomplished a lot, I see."

She gave him a smile. "*Wí.* But there's much more to do."

They stood in silence while the clock on the wall ticked off several seconds, then they both spoke at once.

"Did you want some lunch?"

"I brought your bag out."

She laughed outright, and Trip chuckled nervously, waving for her to go first.

"I could make you a ham sandwich if you're hungry," she said as she made a move toward the fridge.

"I ate up at the house." He gestured toward the floor at his feet. "That's why Momma sent me down with your bag. Do you need a tour of the cabin, or did you figure out where everything is?"

She lifted a hand toward the cabin. "It feels a little awkward, like invading someone's home."

Trip shuffled his feet as he looked beyond her at the closed door. "I reckon it would. Esmeralda lived here for nearly twenty years, and she left in pretty short order. I never checked, is everything okay?"

"*Mo çé bon.* Just some clothes left in the wardrobe, but I have little so I need very little space. And—" She'd been about to say she wasn't going to be staying long, but something made her stop. It wouldn't do to have her employer thinking she'd cut out on him at a moment's notice.

He didn't seem to notice her hesitation. "I can take her things and put them in storage if you want. I think Momma would agree to that. I mean, we wouldn't want the moths to take over or anything." He stooped to pick up her bag and crossed the room to bring it to her. "Why don't you show me what we're looking at."

She led the way back to the cabin door and walked through again. "Did the boy sleep on the futon?"

"Yeah. Jose is a good kid, though not a lot of ambition. Early twenties, done with school. He liked to play video games when he wasn't helping his mom."

"I suppose it's rather typical of the generation," she said, somewhat dismissively.

"Maybe. I always thought he was just a little easygoing. Down Syndrome, you know. Loveable and hardworking, as long as he knows the routine."

Savannah was impressed Trip was so accepting of a characteristic many considered a disability. It spoke well for the kind of person he was.

She smiled over her shoulder at him as she led the way into the bedroom.

chapter
five

Trip followed Savannah—Dawn, he reminded himself—and set her bag down on the end of the bed. She opened the wardrobe to show him the contents, and he tried to focus on her words as she spoke. Something about her clothing being able to fit without a problem. In all honesty, he felt awkward being so close to her in proximity of a bed, and he was wrestling to keep his attention on the problem at hand.

"No, we'll want you to feel right at home," he said. "Esmeralda will understand if we store her stuff."

They stood in another awkward silence while Trip tried to decide what to say and do. He hadn't felt this clumsy around a woman since high school. Mainly because, for the most part, he'd stayed away from them since Kate. He had an easy relationship with Jules, but that was because they didn't want anything from each other except physical relief. Every other woman he managed to keep at a distance the length of the Lazy J's driveway.

He didn't know what was going on with him. Savannah Dawn was the first woman to tease any kind of life into him, and it left him unsure of his footing. The physical attraction was undeniable. She was beautiful, sure, and hard-working, based on all the work she'd done in the kitchen, but he'd seen flashes of something else too. A kind of vulnerability at odds with the moments of confusion her rapid-fire storytelling created in him.

As though she knew more of what was going on with him than he did, she took a step even closer to him and put her hand on his sleeve in a feather-light touch, smiled as he looked down at her, and said something he didn't understand. What had she said the language was? Louisiana Creole? It was low, melodic, and brought to mind artwork he'd seen on some public broadcast show. Rodin's "The Kiss", or Rosso Emerald Crimson's "What Are We Waiting For?".

He shook his head to clear it and said, "I don't understand."

She gave a smile he couldn't read and removed her hand. "I shouldn't say such things. It's not wise of me to tease. . . about someone I don't know."

He was pretty sure what she'd said hadn't had anything to do with Esmeralda. He cleared his throat, feeling out of his depth.

"I guess we could take the hanging clothes up to the guest room at the main house," he said. "The closet up there is plenty big. And you won't need the chest, right? Do you have anything else in your car that needs to come inside?"

"No," she said, taking a step back. "I travel very light these days."

Something in her tone had changed, making him look twice at her. All hints of playfulness had left. She was looking at her hands, which she held clasped in front of her.

"Savannah, I—"

"Please, call me Dawn. It really is quite important."

It was his turn to offer a small smile. "I'll try. It's just…. Savannah suits you so much better." She looked up at him, and the distress he saw in her eyes made him want to retract his statement. "I'm sorry. I really will try. What I was going to say, Miss Dawn, is you're safe here. You should know that. You've got the Thomas family on your side. We won't let anyone hurt you."

That brought a smile back to her face, but it still didn't quite reach her eyes. She took a quick step close to him and tiptoed to place a kiss on his cheek. "*Mersi*, Colton. You're sweet."

His cheeks warmed. "Just you let me know if there's ever anything I can do for you."

And that was pretty much the end of that discussion, as Jax walked into the kitchen looking for something to eat. While Savannah Dawn fixed him a sandwich, Trip corralled him into helping him haul the hanging clothes up to the house. By the time they got back, Jeff and Deke were also there, introducing themselves and accepting plates with a hearty-looking sandwich garnished with Momma's dill pickles. It was almost enough to tempt him into having a second lunch.

As he went about the rest of his day, he found his thoughts straying back to the beautiful woman with the haunting eyes, and he wondered what her story really was. Momma had been less than forthcoming, leaving him to speculate on his own.

Before he could ask her to make him a sandwich—the fellas were all groaning with so much pleasure, he found himself salivating a touch—Blue walked in and made eye contact with him.

"Braxton's on the phone," his brother said. "He wants to know what you plan to do about yesterday."

Trip sighed and reached for his hat, reminded of how he had spent his morning after he got back from his early ride out to the fence line in question.

"He'll just have to wait until I hear back from the fellas down at the marketplace, won't he? He's crazier than a hen with a rattler in the coop if he thinks I'm going to just take his word for it on the market price for what he lost."

Blue leveled a compassionate look at him, then stole a pickle off Jax's plate, much to the young man's annoyance.

"Things like that make me all the more happy you're fixin' to take over around here," Blue said. "That kind of nonsense would send me through the roof."

"I'm not thrilled about it either, little brother. But one of us has to learn how to deal with the hard stuff."

Blue put his hand to his heart as though wounded by Trip's words, but they both knew Trip was right. Blue had no interest whatsoever in the finer points of managing a ten-thousand-acre cattle ranch.

As he left the chow hall, he settled his hat on his head and crossed the yard to the house where his phone call waited.

IT WAS WELL past dark when Savannah finally looked around and conceded she was going to have to leave some things undone before bed.

She was exhausted, but she'd washed and dried her own clothes and started into the mountain belonging to the various ranch hands. Maddy had helped her with another meal—steak and potatoes again—and complimented her on the progress she'd made with the kitchen and chow hall. Every surface was cleaned to her satisfaction, including the bathroom. Really, the only thing left was the laundry.

Maddy knocked on the frame of the door to the kitchen that let out onto a porch facing the main house and stepped inside.

"How are you feeling about breakfast? Do you need any help getting it under control?"

"Kelsey brought more eggs from the farm, and I have bacon thawing in the refrigerator," Savannah said. "I don't know how often you go to the grocery, but I believe we'll need bread soon."

Maddy smiled. "You keep up the good work, and I'll be able to get back to my baking schedule. We don't usually buy bread in. I bake it instead."

"Oh, very good. I thought to make quiche tomorrow instead of scrambled eggs. I have pastry dough already freezing."

"Sounds lovely," Maddy said as she pulled a stool out from under the edge of the counter island and settled onto it. "How are you feeling about the job?"

Savannah gave a little shrug and pulled out a stool on the opposite side. "It's hard work, but good. I think it'll be easier now that . . . ," she paused, and rephrased her next words, "now that I know where everything is."

Maddy laughed. "You mean, now that you've cleaned everything and can keep it that way? Don't worry, Dawn, I know I wasn't staying on top of everything. I'm just happy to have you on board."

"I hope I didn't scare Carson off," she said. "I gave him vigorous demonstration on how to properly wash dishes. No more just washing the inside."

"If you get the message to stick, it will be a first. He's been told many times, but I was never able to stay and supervise him."

"I watched him like a hawk tonight. Made him re-wash several dishes until they were clean enough. I'll make a fine dishwasher out of him. . . if he comes back."

She and Maddy both chuckled, then fell into a weary silence.

"As I said, I'm happy to have you," Maddy began after a few moments, "but I need to know what you're running from. How much trouble are you in?"

The very blunt, direct question caught her completely off guard. She tried to remember what she'd said before, but she hadn't really kept track of her story. She hadn't stayed in any one place long enough to tell her lies more than once.

"You said your husband was looking for you," Maddy prompted. "Is he a violent man? Has he been in trouble with the law? I ask because we recently had some trouble with one of the hands who had an ex-girlfriend show up. Someone died. It's not that we'll turn you away if that's the case," she added hastily, "I'd just like to be prepared."

Savannah took a deep breath. "I'm so sorry you had such trouble. To be honest, I don't know what he's capable of." That, at least, was the truth. Laurencett had betrayed her, the cost of which was unknown and likely deadly. "He's never physically hurt me, but I've seen horrible things. I came a long way from home to escape him. I don't think he'd expect to see me in a place like this. He thinks of me as a city girl."

"Ah," Maddy said, the frown clearing from her face.

Savannah wanted to change the topic before the older woman realized she was holding back information. She didn't know yet if she was safe enough to tell Maddy the whole story. Not to mention, if she did tell and Laurencett found her here, not one person on this ranch would be safe from the consequences. It had nothing to do with trust and everything to do with power and resources the Thomas family would never be able to withstand.

She stifled a huge yawn and forced herself to stand. "I wanted to do more of the washing, but I'm dead on my feet."

Maddy stood as well. "Don't let me keep you up. You want me to check in on you in the morning?"

"I saw an alarm clock in the bedroom I can set. What time is sunrise?"

"The boys will be up at six o'clock, so plan accordingly. If you need anything, just stand on the porch and holler," she said with a smile.

Savannah gave a tired, but genuine laugh. "*Mersi*, Maddy. *Bonswá*."

"Goodnight, dear. Sleep well."

The door closed with a click behind the older woman, and Savannah sighed and turned to the cabin. She had opened the windows to let in the evening breeze and decided the room had cooled off nicely as she washed her face and braided her hair in a loose plait for bed.

When she turned back the covers and crawled in, her limbs felt so heavy and exhaustion crowded the corners of her mind enough, she thought perhaps this night she would not have bad dreams.

EMMANUEL LAURENCETT PAUSED JUST inside the door of the Antebellum-style mansion and straightened his tie before buttoning his jacket. It was cool inside, a relief from the wet, sticky evening air. Glancing in a mirror, he smoothed a wayward curl of his short, black hair away from his face, then gave an artful tug to make just the front stand up in a fashionable tousle.

He wasn't looking forward to this interview. Nothing had been going right on this case, and now he had to report—again—that there was no news.

The butler—a stereotypical black butler who could have walked right off the set of "Gone with the Wind" or "Django Unchained"—motioned for him to come, and he followed the man into the parlor off to the left.

Not the office. That was a good sign she was in a decent mood.

The parlor was a lush homage to pre-Civil War plantations, with meticulously maintained Louis XIV furniture, gilded crown molding, and framed paintings on the wall worth more than Laurencett could probably earn in a decade on the job. Not that *she* would ever dream of selling them.

"Madame," he said, bowing stiffly to the woman who sat in a high-backed giltwood armchair as if it were a throne. He took note of the small frown that pinched her brows and quickly corrected himself. "Mama Sanci."

Laurencett was aware he was tacitly uninvited to sit, given all the chairs were turned so none faced her, and to sit would be to put himself out of position to address her directly.

"Tell me you have news," she said without preamble.

"I'm afraid not, Madame. For all intents, she's vanished."

"That's unacceptable, boy." The words were hard, the voice behind them harder. Mama Sanci leaned forward, her eyes like chipped emeralds against the light brown tones of her face. "Reach out to every avenue available to you. I want her found. Fail to do so, and I'll see you on the wrong end of an alligator hunt in the swamp."

Waving a hand to dismiss him, she said something in that bastardized French language of hers, and the butler extended his arm in a gesture that clearly meant it was time to leave. He was all too happy to oblige.

If something didn't break soon, he needed to come up with his own exit strategy.

chapter
six

Savannah jerked awake, sitting straight up in bed, her heart hammering in her chest. The dream was the same as always, the inexorable train wreck her life had become. The accusation, the threat, the escape, capture, and—dear God—Dion's face moments before . . . . She inhaled sharply and rubbed her eyes with the heels of her hands.

This couldn't go on, could it? Must she work herself into a coma before she got a good night's sleep?

She flopped back against the pillows and listened to the night sounds for a time, trying to determine whether something else had awoken her. All was quiet. Even the crickets had gone to sleep for the night. The clock on the table told her it was 2:00 AM. She still had some time to try to get back to sleep, but she felt wide awake.

To pass the time and attempt to make something useful out of being awake, she tried to picture each of the ranch hands she'd met so far and place names with faces.

Jax was easy. He was a sweet young man who had the look of a haunted soul when he wasn't actively interacting with her. She figured she'd have to ask him if she wanted to find out more about that.

Then there was Jeff, the taciturn wrangler, and Tim, his helper in the barn. Deke was the generous foreman, and then there were the surly twins, Ray and Rick. Pete and the one they called a rookie, Ned. Kelsey was from the farm up the road. There were others, but she couldn't bring any more to mind.

Her eyes drifted shut at last, and her breath puffed out evenly as she tried to count the many different faces she had seen just since coming out to this ranch—this haven from the dangers of the road. That was one thing Mrs. Thomas hadn't been wrong about. She *was* in danger, but she feared she would never find anyone who could truly help her in the long run. Not even here.

By the time the alarm went off, she had managed to fall into a trance of sorts, enough that she felt moderately rested. She wrestled herself free of the covers and stumbled to the bathroom, emerging ten minutes later fully dressed and ready to start her day. Well…ready to get a pot of coffee on so she could get ready to start her day.

Fumbling her way into the dark kitchen, she thought she saw movement outside the window and froze, her heart in her throat. She wished she'd turned the light off in the cabin before she came through. Anyone outside might see her silhouetted against the light from the other room.

A man walked across the big open space between the main house and the barn. When he turned his head, she realized it was Trip and sagged against the drainboard counter, strength sapped by that moment of terror.

He walked to the barn and disappeared inside, so she went through the motions of brewing the first pot of coffee. By the time she had the initial batch of pie dough out, he was back, mounting a horse and riding past on his way up the road. He looked inside, saw her watching, and tipped his hat to her.

Where on earth was he going at this hour?

It wasn't a puzzle she had any time or resources to solve. The clock was ticking on breakfast, and she had no desire to have hungry cowboys waiting on her to provide them with the most important meal of the day.

As TRIP PASSED the chow hall on his way back to the barn, he smelled something heavenly wafting from the building. Without realizing his own intentions, he urged Scotchie over and dismounted by the steps, tossing the reins over the porch railing. Scotchie was too well-trained not to stay put. Before he could open the door, it swung open and the rest of the boys piled out, heading for the barn.

Blue was the last to exit, munching on some last bite of food most likely stolen from someone else's plate. The smile on his brother's face was telling. Whatever he'd cadged, he liked it.

"Whatcha got there, Blue?" he asked.

His brother put his hand in front of his mouth and grunted barely intelligible words at him. "Quiche. Bacon. Good." He swallowed. "I think Miss Dawn is going to see a lot more of me. My wife isn't a bad cook, but her repertoire is limited. This . . . ." He popped a last morsel in his mouth and sighed.

"Well heck, is there any left?"

"Dunno. You'll have to check with Miss Dawn." Blue patted him on the shoulder as he passed, on his way over to the office in the main house.

Trip crossed the threshold and surveyed the room,

looking for any leftovers in the chaos of the deserted table. He didn't find any, but as he heard Savannah Dawn rattling dishes in the kitchen, he felt bad the rest of the hands had just abandoned her to take care of the mess they'd left. He gathered a few plates and some silverware and headed for the swinging door, barely dodging in time when she pushed through with a purpose.

"Oh!" she said, putting her hand to her breast in shock. "*Bondjé!* I thought everyone had gone."

"I'm sorry, ma'am. I just came looking for some of that quiche. It smells so good. Then I saw the mess the fellas left you and thought I'd help out."

"*Mersi*," she said, and reached for the plates he held. "I can get them."

"Let me help," he said, pulling the plates out of her reach. "It ain't nothing." She looked up at him, protest in her green eyes, but he didn't back down. "It's the least I can do for coming in so late."

She hesitated, then nodded and turned to the table to collect more dishes. He pushed through the door and held it open for her, then followed her to the sink. They made several more trips in silence, then she pulled a pie dish out from under a towel where it had been cooling on the island counter. She served him a slice before Trip thought of something to say.

"That isn't your breakfast, is it?"

She finally smiled at him. "I made extra in case the men were very hungry. This'd be lunch if not breakfast. You enjoy. It's better hot, but still good cold."

He spotted bacon and what looked suspiciously like spinach layered under the cheesy eggs, inside a flaky and golden crust. He accepted the fork she held out and cut into it as he settled onto the stool. She watched as he took the bite, the same way she'd watched him with the sweet potato soup, like she expected him to fall off his chair in shock.

As he bit into the savory morsel, he allowed he might just fall off his chair if he were prone to dramatics.

"Yum," he said, then couldn't believe he'd said that out loud. He tried to catch back some of his dignity. "This is very good. What's that flavor in there? It's more than just bacon, cheese, and spinach."

She reached out and tapped his nose before turning to the sink. "The secret's in the spice."

He watched her for a moment, still feeling the gentle tap of her finger as he enjoyed the view from his position. Then he mentally reeled himself in and ate a few more bites, trying to identify the flavors dancing on his tongue. His mom was a good cook, but Savannah's way with spices illustrated what a different world she came from.

"Where'd you learn to cook?" he asked as he scraped his fork across the dish in an effort to collect the last possible crumb.

Without turning to him, she shrugged. "*Mo moman*, my mother. She loved to cook. When I was small, I helped her in the kitchen every day."

Savannah Dawn's shoulders shook with the vigor she applied to the dishes, and Trip noticed she'd stiffened. If she were a horse, he'd say she'd been spooked by something. He picked up his dirty dishes and brought them to the sink, peering around to see her face.

She quickly raised an arm and pressed her cheek against her shoulder, wiping a tear from the corner of her eye.

"You okay?" he asked.

She gave a shaky laugh. "I splashed water in my eye. It's nothing."

"Sa...Miss Dawn," he began, and she ducked her head to her work.

"I'm just tired. I didn't sleep so well, being in a strange bed. I'm fine."

He didn't buy it. She did look tired, but she'd been fine until he'd asked her a personal question. Rather than herd her into a corner, he backed off. "Tell you what," he said, "I'll come by tonight with a bottle of my special hooch and we'll have a drink together. That might help us both sleep."

She looked up at him with a smile of genuine relief. "I saw you early this morning. Where do you go before the sun comes up?"

It was his turn to shrug. "I go up the hill, watch the sunrise. It's a peaceful time of day, before the chores need doing, before anyone else is up—besides you, of course." He smiled at her. "When I can't sleep, I go up to the rim of the hollow and try to put my thoughts to rest. I guess you could say it's a kind of meditation."

"Ah," she said, a sad smile lighting her eyes. "I should meditate. I used to practice before . . . ."

He waited for her to continue but she didn't, just resumed scrubbing stubborn cheese off the plates. "Well, maybe some morning you'll fix something up that doesn't have to be served hot and I'll take you up with me."

"On your horse?" she asked, a mixture of gratitude and pleasure in her voice. "I'd like that."

The thought of Savannah Dawn riding in front of him sent a thrill through him. He didn't trust himself to speak for a moment. "Sure," he said at last, just as he caught movement across the yard. His father had stepped out onto the porch and was looking over at Scotchie with a frown. "Whoops, I gotta go. Daddy's looking for me. I'll catch you later tonight, all right?"

He waited for her nod in acknowledgement, then spun

on his heel and headed for the door. "Thanks again for breakfast, Miss Dawn."

SAVANNAH WATCHED Trip dash down the stairs and cross the yard with a ground-eating stride—the same stride she'd seen that morning as he walked to the barn. He just wasn't the sort to let the grass grow under his feet. All his movements were quick and purposeful, even when he was ostensibly relaxing.

She shook her head. He was filled with pent up energy, and because he directed it into forward, positive motion, it was an attractive quality. It reminded her more than a little of Dion.

At that thought, she closed her eyes and let the familiar pain wash through her. Poor Dion.

A jolt of pain in the present moment snapped her out of her remorse. She looked down to see she'd cut her finger with the knife she'd been washing. A foolish mistake to lose herself while handling cutlery. She cursed and turned on the cold water, letting it run over the red drop of blood on her index finger as she poked and prodded to see how deep it was. It wasn't too bad. The knife point had not penetrated more than a fraction through the skin. It would probably be done bleeding by the time she finished the dishes.

She bent herself back to the task at hand, intent on finishing the dishes so she could make a trip to Mrs. Thomas's garden. She'd been promised a tour so she'd know what she had to work with for fresh greens.

chapter
seven

Trip paused outside the open door to the sitting room of the main house, a firm grip on the neck of the bottle in his hand. Inside, Momma and Daddy didn't appear to want or need a distraction from the tender kiss they shared.

He smiled. After forty years of marriage, it was sweet they could be so much in love that they kissed like newlyweds. Rather than interrupt, he tiptoed past the doorway and out the front door. He didn't really need to be silent, but he pulled the door closed quietly and eased the screen door into place with only a soft *thunk*.

He walked the path to the chow hall—to Savannah Dawn's cabin—with deliberate and anticipatory steps. He'd argued with himself back and forth for nearly a half hour about whether he should bring her the bottle as he'd promised or just go to bed. In the end, he'd looked out the window of his room, saw her silhouette in the kitchen, and that had been all it took to grab the bottle and head downstairs.

Now, he wasn't so sure again. It didn't mean anything

to bring her a shot of hooch, right? Except the very fact he was having an argument with himself meant it did mean something, he just didn't know what. He was about to turn around again when her voice called out to him from the open window.

"Colton!" His given name on her lips was musical. Musical and dangerous. "Is that your hooch?"

It would have been a silly question if her accent hadn't made it so adorable. So sexy.

"Yes, ma'am." He angled toward the door to her cabin when he saw her wave. "But Colton is my dad." He instinctively knew if he let her keep saying his name like that, it would be impossible to pretend he didn't find her attractive. He lifted the bottle. "Are you still interested?"

"Very much, yes." She was in the doorway now, both inviting him onto the porch and effectively blocking the entrance to the cabin.

"Trip." The lilt of her saying his nickname was still a distraction—still spelled trouble. "Are you called this because you were a clumsy child?"

He laughed, though it was not the first time someone had asked that. "No. With Daddy being Colton Junior, it was just too confusing. I'm Colton the Third. Colton tripled. Trip."

"*Mwen wa*. I see. I like this reason." She put a finger to her chin, almost playfully. "Trip, I've tasted Louisiana hooch before, but never Kansas hooch. I'm curious to taste the difference."

Trip gave the bottle in his hand a glance, surprised he'd never considered there might be a difference in the kinds of hooch one could find around the country.

"A buddy of mine who has a still out on his property made this. He uses corn mash, I think. All I know for sure is it bites like a coyote caught in a beaver trap. You still want?"

She nodded and held out two glass tumblers she'd brought from the kitchen. "I could use a little oblivion tonight, I think."

He poured two fingers of the clear liquid in each glass, then took one from her and settled onto the bench. She sat down beside him but left a good two feet of distance between them. "How come you can't sleep?" he asked at last. "If you don't mind me asking."

She sipped at the glass and gave an involuntary shudder as the strong liquor bit her. She was silent for so long, he began to think she wouldn't answer. "I think because it's too quiet out here. I'm not used to being able to hear the sound of a horse farting in the barn from my bedroom."

Trip laughed at her unexpected statement. "Sound does carry at night, doesn't it? I daresay you'll get used to it. Tim came from Denver, had never been around horses or away from the noise of the city, but he says he loves it out here."

"How did he end up here?" She took another sip and gave him a curious look.

It wasn't lost on Trip that she'd turned his question aside with humor and a smooth change of subject. "His sister married my brother. When he needed a place to come, we worked it out that he could come here. Now he's gone and gotten serious with *my* sister. They've been officially dating for about four months. They seem to be happy."

"*Bon*," she said absently. "I like the happy stories. Know any more?"

"Young Jax is in love with my niece. They've gone

through some sh. . . a real mess together, but now they seem quite happy together, too."

Savannah gave him a sly smile. The flirty vixen side of her personality was back. "So, something in the Kansas air makes people fall in love, yes? Or is it just limited to your little town?"

He knew her observation was a tease, but it made him think. Or maybe the hooch was already kicking in. "I don't know. Whatever it is, it certainly doesn't work on everyone. My fiancée—" His teeth clicked shut. Just that little introduction had him teetering over the black hole that had grown around his heart. He wasn't ready to talk about it.

Savannah scooted closer to him on the bench. "You were to be married?" She lifted his left hand and traced her finger lightly over his bare ring finger. "This says you're still free."

She didn't want me, he didn't say. She wanted her career and her figure more than she wanted kids and the challenge of being a rancher's wife.

"I'm still free," he agreed, hoping his tone would convey his desire to change the subject. He really didn't want to be rude.

"*Bon.* Good," she said, then tipped her glass back, finishing off the shot of liquor. "You seem to be a good man, Colton Thomas the Third. Trip. You deserve to be with someone who wants you."

Trip studied her face, blinking rapidly as he checked his memories to see if he'd said those words out loud. He didn't think so. She seemed to have read his mind. She met his gaze with an unblinking expression, the dark pools of her eyes barely visible in the shadow cast by the porch roof.

"Come, show me why you love it here," she said abruptly, changing the subject yet again. She stood and tugged him to his feet as well. They faced each other, swaying a bit, until she laughed again. "Perhaps that's not such a wise idea. I'm not sure I can walk. Your hooch is very strong."

He grinned. He couldn't help it. "Then my work here is done. Let me help you to your bed, my lady," he said in his most gallant knight voice.

Before she could protest, he tucked an arm just below her shoulders, swept his other arm behind her knees, and picked her up in one smooth movement. She gasped, the look of shock on her face the kind that usually preceded a slap. It was anyone's guess how she was going to react, but Trip thought he was on safe ground when her body relaxed against him.

When she didn't demand to be returned to her feet, he hooked the toe of his boot into a gap between two boards in a corner of the screen door, pried it open and carried her through to the bedroom. Rather than dropping her onto the bed like he very much wanted to do, he gently set her on her feet.

SAVANNAH DIDN'T KNOW what to think. She *couldn't* with the way her mind was buzzing from the drink and the man who had picked her up like she didn't weigh a thing.

The moment her feet touched the ground, she took a small step back and stood facing him, searching his gaze.

There was raw desire in his expression—she was used to seeing that—but he had a tight grip on his control. He was a gentleman, and she could see he would never push her into something she didn't want—not that she didn't feel an answering desire for him.

Trip was a very attractive man, a million miles apart

from the men she was typically required to flirt with. Tanned cheeks, clean-shaven for the evening, chiseled features, earnest blue eyes, short, light brown hair—he looked every inch the working man he was. The way he'd swept her off her feet was textbook fairytale, and she had to admit to the appeal of that kind of physical strength. He filled out his wranglers and button-down work shirt as well as any of the musclemen who graced the covers of romance novels.

Oh yes, given different circumstances, she could easily imagine a fling with this cowboy. But then what?

Before she could travel too far down that rabbit hole, he took another step back from her.

"Miss Savannah. . . Dawn," he said, catching and correcting himself. "I know there's something you're not telling us. I don't need to know what it is, but I'll say it again. I want you to know you're safe out here. We can and will protect our own, and now that you work here, you're one of us. So if you need anything, ever, just let me know and I'll take care of it—I'll take care of you."

His words touched her with their sincerity. Before she could properly react, he turned toward the door. He was halfway through it before she called out to him. "Thank you, Trip. Goodnight."

He turned back to her, then made as if to tip his hat to her. "Goodnight, Miss Dawn."

She trailed after him and watched through the screen door as he crossed the yard, heading into the main house. Then slowly, deliberately, she shut the door. Still pondering his words, she went back to her room and sat on the edge of the bed.

I'll take care of you. The words echoed in her mind, taking her back nearly ten months to another state, another room, another voice saying those same words.

Savannah closed her eyes as the memory of sitting in the shade of the wheelhouse on the yacht surfaced. She could almost feel the winter sunshine reflecting off Lake Pontchartrain.

"I don't see what difference I could make." Savannah adjusted the sunglasses on her nose to peer briefly at the ebony-skinned man leaning against the rail of the eighty-foot luxury yacht with a casual demeanor he was surely far from feeling. "She won't listen to me. She never has."

Dion's smile was a flash of brilliance against the deep brown of his face. "I think you underestimate your influence. You have always been exactly what she wanted you to be. How could she fail to take notice when you finally break free and challenge her?"

"Oh, I don't fear her indifference. I fear she will notice, and when she does, it may destroy me."

"I got your back. I'll take care of you."

Those bold words had spoken to her soul. But were they any more viable now than on that fateful day?

Sitting alone in the little cabin, Savannah raised her hands to her cheeks, the warmth of that winter day a memory on her skin. Wasn't that the point where everything had started to go wrong?

What if she hadn't fallen for Dion's charms? What if she hadn't brought him on the cruise? What if she hadn't listened to him? Would she still be back in New Orleans, safe and comfortable? Clueless?

At the very least, Dion would still be alive, and she wouldn't have a price on her head.

With slow, measured movements, she slipped out of her clothes and into her pajamas, then crawled between the sheets and lay her head against the cool pillowcase.

For once, the last waking thought she had was not of Dion and his fragile-looking academic's frame, but rather

Trip, in his work clothes, steady and strong. Of the two, she imagined Trip stood a better chance of surviving the hurricane she was sure dogged her heels. The hurricane Dion had not survived.

chapter
eight

When Trip returned to the house, all the lights were off except a thin line beneath the door to the master suite where his parents would be readying for bed. A glance at the grandfather clock in the hall told him while it wasn't especially late, it would be smart if he went straight up to bed.

With as little sleep as he'd been getting, another sleepless night would strip him down to nothing. And he couldn't afford to be nothing. He never could, even on his darkest days. His position on the ranch meant he had daily duties that could not be neglected, no matter how he was feeling.

Thankfully, the hooch seemed to be doing its thing. He savored the slight wobble to his steps and heaviness of his eyelids. Sleep should hit the same moment his head hit the pillow.

What a nice change from the way his nights had been falling out recently.

Up in his room, his teeth brushed and orange pajama bottoms replacing his jeans, he threw back the covers and hopped into bed. He hugged his pillow beneath him and thought about Savannah Dawn. He knew as much as she had told Momma, about being on the run from an abusive husband, but that didn't sit quite right with him. She didn't seem like she had been abused—he'd known a few women who had endured bad marriages, and they'd all been shy and reserved.

Savannah Dawn had her moments of shyness to be sure, but she'd also had moments where she flirted with him, teasing the way the abused women he'd known never would have. Not that he was under the illusion he knew everything about the way people behaved—everyone dealt with stress in their own unique way.

But Savannah . . . . How could she be so confident and still be afraid? She'd played with his head, confusing him with conflicting stories. She'd aroused his curiosity. She'd accepted an invitation to ride with him and drank hooch with him. And yet, she'd cried at the mere mention of her mother. There had been real fear in her eyes when she'd said she was in danger.

He heaved a sigh into his pillow and hugged it a little tighter to himself, wishing he was holding her . . . . He'd picked her up and carried her into her room on a whim, but now he couldn't shake the feel of her, or the desire to have her in his arms again.

Lord, I'm a mess. The only way he was going to get her out of his system was if he found out more about her. That, or avoid her like a pig running from the slaughter-house. Somehow, that didn't seem like it was going to be practical.

He rolled onto his back so he could stare at the ceiling, but his eyes kept drifting closed. It was time to stop fighting sleep—time to let go so he could start tomorrow with a fresh mind.

SAVANNAH WAS PLEASED at the way she fell into her work over the next few days. Mornings started early, cooking hearty meals the men required to fuel their days. She spent a little bit of time getting to know the ranch hands and learning their preferences, then, like every good cook she'd ever known, she began infiltrating the meals with her own unique style and palate.

Most of her first two days had been filled with laundry, laundry, and more laundry. She'd gotten a crash course from Maddy in removing sweat stains from shirts and animal hair and mud from jeans, and learned the men's sizes so she could sort the clean clothes for each man.

When not cooking or catching up on the laundry, she'd spent time exploring her new domain and making it her own. She'd organized the cupboards to her satisfaction and learned what spices and ingredients she had on hand. She made lists of the things she needed in order to put her own stamp on the foods she cooked and had taken a trip up to the west end of the property to see the farm and learn what resources she had there.

It was daunting, but she found she loved it. The sheer freshness of the ingredients made her cooking come alive, and though the men claimed resistance to change, she began to offer one altered dish with each meal, each of which were met with vocal praise.

Once she put the fear of re-washing every dinner dish into Carson, she found her evenings very enjoyable indeed. She watched the activities of the ranch winding down from her spot on the porch while the sun set in the west, then made final preparations for the morning meals before collapsing into bed. She began to appreciate the quiet of the ranch, and after the night Trip had put her to bed, she had little trouble falling into a sleep so deep, her dreams couldn't find her.

The Saturday of that first week, just four long days since her arrival, she was enjoying what might well be her last evening free of dish duty—Carson was going back to school next week, and his parents had refused to let him continue his summer job—when Trip rode up.

She hadn't seen much of him since they'd shared shots of hooch. She smiled at him in the hopes he would come see her. To her pleasure, he angled the horse and came to a stop in front of her porch step. Savannah smiled and stood up to pet the horse's nose in greeting.

"Miss Dawn." Trip sounded tired.

"Trip," she said back. "I think I have a carrot I can get for your horse." She reached a hand out to smooth down the nose of the animal, which snorted at her, wet enough to coat her hand in slobber.

"Scotchie!" Trip said, and twitched the reins lightly, just enough to make the horse lift his head in apology—or defiance. "He heard the c-word. The greedy gut is hoping you'll run and fetch him some food. Next he'll try to convince you I never feed him."

She smiled as she looked down the sleek length of the animal's side. The beast was well-muscled and fit—a lot like his rider. "It would take a lot to convince me of this. He's beautiful."

Trip chuckled and leaned forward until his forearm rested on the pommel of the saddle. He looked about ready to say something, then he sat up. "I've got to get him inside," he said, and she had the distinct impression that was not what he had first intended. "It's been a long day."

"I found a bottle of wine," she said. "If you'd like to unwind, come share it with me."

He gazed at her for a long moment, then nodded before turning Scotchie's head toward the barn. "I might just do that," he said over his shoulder. "Thank you."

She wasn't sure why she'd invited him to share the wine, except for the fact that she was lonely. She had been lonely for the better part of the last year. Since her arrival, Maddy had given her some company during the day, but most of the time she was left to her own devices, and she wanted someone to talk with. Someone approachable and handsome, so she could pretend everything was normal for a while.

She was still sitting on the porch a short while later when Trip came up out of the barn. He was very tired, she decided upon seeing the absence of his normal ground-eating stride. He was practically trudging toward her up the slight rise.

"Have you eaten?" she asked abruptly. "You look *harasé*, exhausted."

He looked confused for a moment, then swept off his hat and rubbed a hand through his shock of brown hair. "I've been dealing with the neighbor the last couple days."

"The one who had cows in his fields?" she asked, remembering back to her first night at the ranch.

"That's the one. He's kept me on my toes, but I think we're in the home stretch. I had an independent appraiser out today who's drawing up an estimate of the damages. Once he turns that in, we can let the insurance companies settle it."

"Will he be satisfied with the estimate?"

"He better be. He agreed on the choice of appraiser." He slapped at his thighs, raising a cloud of dust. "I haven't eaten, but I haven't cleaned up either."

She had the feeling if she waited for him to go to the

main house, she wouldn't get him back out to join her. "This is not a problem, Trip. Come, I'll feed you."

He hesitated for the briefest of moments, then climbed the two steps to her porch and followed her inside. He toed off his boots, then gestured to the bathroom. "May I wash my hands in your sink?"

"But of course." She washed her own hands, then lit a burner under the cast iron skillet and busied herself pulling ingredients out of the refrigerator. By the time she had an omelet well under way, he was back. She could tell he'd washed his face and doused his head under the water. His hair and the collar of his shirt were damp, but his face looked a bit more refreshed.

Savannah smiled and gestured for him to sit on one of the stools at the island. "Sit. Food will be ready in a moment."

He sighed as he pulled out a stool. When she turned back to him after checking the pan, she was struck by the intimacy of having him in her kitchen. It gave her pause, wondering how many women over the centuries had been in her shoes, bringing food to a hard-working man . . . .

The very idea was one hundred eighty degrees from any experience of her life so far. Sure, she'd cooked for people, but it had always been for parties as part of the social life she'd been forced to leave behind. Her mother had loved to brag about her cooking skills, and her dishes had been featured at dozens of events each year, from small, intimate parties to larger balls and banquets. But this job had already pushed her skills to grow. Three meals daily for eight to ten men was a world away from one or two dishes for a single weekend event.

And now, cooking for one man while he sat there watching her every move…. It was not only intimate, she found it sexy as hell.

chapter
nine

S avannah Dawn stared at Trip with a faraway look in her eye that both pleased him and kind of freaked him out. There was an odd sort of longing to the tilt of her head and the sad little frown on her lips, and he wondered what she was really thinking about. He doubted it was him.

"You said you had some wine?" he said, to break the tension mounting within him. She shook her head slightly, as if realizing she'd been staring.

"Oh, *wi*. It's there, in the door of the refrigerator."

He nodded and stood to cross the room and fetch it, needing something to occupy himself. "Would you like me to open it?"

"*Mersi*." She pulled open a drawer in the kitchen island and extracted a corkscrew before turning back to the stove to tend the skillet. As he began to peel the foil from the neck of the bottle, she spoke over her shoulder at him. "I'm not familiar with the vintage," she said, "It's not old, so I don't think it's anything special. And don't know if Esmeralda knows anything about wine. I suppose we'll find out, *wi?*"

Trip looked at the label. It was a Sauvignon Blanc. "I suppose we will. I didn't even know Esmeralda drank, but I guess in retrospect it doesn't surprise me. She was a very laid-back woman. I prefer beer, but if I'm going to drink wine, I find a white to be a pleasant substitute."

He uncorked the bottle, then set it aside to let it breathe.

Savannah Dawn hummed a little as she served an omelet up on a plate with quick, sure movements. When she turned to present him with the plate, he took it with a smile.

"It looks great," he said, and it really did. The cheese was perfectly melted, the folded surface perfectly browned.

She shrugged. "It's just eggs and cheese with a little chives. Simple."

"For you, maybe. I couldn't find my way around a kitchen, even with a boy scout to guide me."

She laughed, and it was a beautiful sound. "No, surely not. I think Maddy would have taught you at least to make eggs."

Trip shook his head. "I spend most of my waking hours in the saddle. When it's time to eat, I'm in front of a plate, not a stove. Unless we're talking campfires. Momma never tried to get me into the kitchen." He forked up a small mountain of omelet and took a bite. The eggs were fluffy and perfect, and there was a flavor to them he couldn't pinpoint. Savory and a little spicy.

"There's more than cheese and chives in this," he said, pointing his fork at her.

She laughed again. "I tell you too many times already, it's the spice. If you want to know my secrets, you must come cook with me."

"I think your secrets are about more than your cooking," he said, then checked himself by eating another mouthful. He hurried to think of something to curb the look of alarm growing on her face. "I think Esmeralda left a hidden arsenal of spices she never used for us and you found it, all unknowing."

It was a lame coverup, but she smiled hesitantly and appeared to give him the benefit of the doubt. She covered her own reaction by going to a cupboard and bringing down two wine glasses. Pouring a small amount into one, she offered it to Trip.

"Test," she said. "Make sure it goes with your eggs."

He took the glass and, pretending to be a sommelier, sniffed it, then sipped, letting it roll around on his tongue to mingle with the taste of the omelet. He hadn't been expecting much—eggs were an oddball item to pair wine with—but . . . .

"It actually works," he said. "I had my doubts."

"You know much about wine?"

"Not especially. But I know what I like." He met and held her gaze for a moment before she looked away, her cheeks heating to a slightly darker shade than her normal warm brown. She was blushing.

Savannah Dawn covered her discomfort by pouring more wine in his glass, then filling one for herself. After she scrubbed the skillet clean and applied a thin coat of oil, she leaned her hip against the island counter across from him while he made quick work of the omelet. It had been huge, five or six eggs, but he ate every bite.

"I guess I was hungrier than I thought," he said, then raised his wine glass to her. "Thank you."

"It was my pleasure." She raised her own glass in a kind of unspoken salute. They watched each other almost awkwardly for a moment, then she stood up straight. "Do you play poker?"

The question came from so far out of the blue that he

just blinked at her for a moment. "Poker?"

"*Wi*. The card game? I found some playing cards in the cabin and I desire to play with someone tonight. I haven't taken much time to have fun since I got here. It's Saturday night, after all. Maddy said even you take Sunday mornings off."

"True," he said.

Sleeping in was not an activity he normally engaged in, but on Sundays he had nothing scheduled until church at 9:00AM.

"Then come," Savannah said, taking her glass and the bottle of wine into the cabin.

Trip hesitated a moment longer, then put his dishes to soak in the sink before grabbing his glass and following. She was settling onto the futon when he entered and he paused, not sure where to sit. She patted the cushion next to her, then refilled both their glasses before setting the bottle on the low coffee table.

"What's your game?" he asked, not sure if he was talking about the cards or trying to ferret out any ulterior motive.

"Did you know five card stud was created in New Orleans?" she countered, shuffling the deck against the space between them on the futon. "For me, it's the only way to play *poque*."

"*Poque?* You mean poker?"

"*Wi, poque* is the original name of the game. But maybe you're scared to play this game. Maybe you think you can't win against me."

"There you go again, daring me to do things your way," he said in return.

She laughed. "But you always accept my dare, yes?"

"Touché." He picked up the cards she dealt him one at a time. "So, do you play this straight or with wild cards?"

"Wild *card*," she corrected. "Just one. My uncle always chastised me for playing with a wild, but I like the added spice of uncertainty."

Trip decided that statement held true for more than just cards when it came to Savannah Dawn.

"Dealer's choice on the wild card then," he said. "What are we wagering?"

"I like the one-eyed jack of hearts, I think. As for wagers. . . I suppose we can keep points? I have no cash, I just want to play."

"Points it is."

SAVANNAH LEANED against the back of the futon, her cards clutched close to her chest as she studied Trip, watching for any clue as to what he had in his hand. She may have met her match. He had foiled her at every turn, and the points on his side of the notepad far outstripped hers.

"It's a good thing we don't play for anything more than points," she said, tossing her cards down onto the cushion. "I fold, and I'm done, I think."

Trip set his cards down, and she reached to turn them over to learn if he had been bluffing. His warm hand covered hers, holding it and the cards down.

"Nuh-uh," he said, his tone mock-serious. "You gotta pay to peek. We already went over this."

"But I'm giving up. You win," she protested. "Besides, what have I to pay you with?" She looked up at him as she spoke, and saw his eyes dilate at some thought.

"I'm sure I could come up with something," he said, his voice low and thoughtful.

"*Bondjé!*" she exclaimed, catching sight of the clock as

she sought a distraction. "Is that the time?" They'd been playing for hours, and while she truly was surprised it was almost midnight, her exclamation was as much a diversion as a true concern.

When Trip looked up to check the clock, she snatched the cards out from under his hand and turned them up so she could see.

"You *were* bluffing!" she said. "I knew it!"

"Did not!" he said, grasping at the cards and succeeding in capturing her wrist. "You would have called if you knew."

She pulled her hand close, and his hand came with it, causing him to lean toward her until he crossed into her personal space. It was not an unpleasant invasion. They stared at each other for a moment. Every laugh they'd shared in the past few hours, every joke, every dare, every bluff, every triumph, every loss…it had all served to create a bond of friendship she felt growing between them. And all that bond was stretched as she contemplated her next move.

She wanted to kiss him, and she was sure he wanted to kiss her. She'd seen that look in many men's eyes, but none of those men had been her boss. She wasn't sure a kiss wasn't crossing a line of some kind.

Before she could act on it or worry too much about it, he sat back and made a show of counting up points on the notepad. "It's too bad we weren't playing for more than points," he said. "I cleaned house on you."

She leaned her elbow against the back of the futon and gazed at him with a smile. "I admit it," she said. "I under-estimated you."

He leaned back as well, and their gazes locked, just a couple feet of cushion separating them.

"You wouldn't be the first." He reached out to run the

corner of a card against the back of her hand in a light circular pattern. She saw it was the jack of hearts, the one that had turned up as their wild card in more than one hand. She let her eyes close, enjoying the sensation of touch on her skin.

When it stopped she didn't open her eyes, even when the cushion shifted as Trip moved. She half expected him to lean in and kiss her. It was a moment before she realized he had climbed to his feet, the clink of glass betraying his movement toward the kitchen with their glasses and the empty bottle.

"Trip?" she asked, without knowing what she planned to say.

"Goodnight, Miss Dawn," he said with slight hesitation, as though he had to think about what name to call her by. It was a bit of a jolt to hear her assumed name, a cold reminder she couldn't let herself get attached, no matter her attraction to Trip.

"Goodnight," she said, and pushed herself to her feet to follow. She needed to make sure the kitchen was properly shut down for the night. He cast a look over his shoulder as he paused on the threshold to the porch to push his feet into his boots. He tipped his hat to her and pulled the door closed behind him, leaving her alone. Just like that.

She went to the window and watched him cross the yard and enter the main house. Moments later a light shone in an upstairs window, throwing his shadow against the curtains.

Feeling a little pervy, she turned away and checked to make sure the stove was off and she had put everything away. It took just a moment to wash the dishes from Trip's meal, then there was nothing to do but go to bed.

Go to bed and try not to dream about a certain sexy

cowboy.

chapter
ten

Momma's elbow in Trip's ribs woke him to the fact that everyone in the church was rising to sing after the sermon ended. He quickly joined them, singing on automatic, the hymn one he knew by heart. His mind was a million miles away, lost in the gaze of a green-eyed woman, where it had been since the night before.

It was a kind of enchantment. The more he tried to forget about her, the more his mind came back to her. He'd had fun playing cards with her, especially winning. She was such a poor loser.

Momma nudged him again, and he realized the hymn was over, the pews were beginning to clear, and Momma was annoyed he hadn't been paying attention. In the pew behind them, however, Blue was amused.

"It's a thin line between Saturday night and Sunday morning, ain't it, brother?" he said, earning his own nudge from his wife.

"Blue, be nice," Mitzi said.

Blue just chuckled and gestured for her to precede him out into the aisle, giving her baby bump a little pat as she sidled by him. They had announced her pregnancy just a week ago.

Trip could tell by the look on Blue's face he was in for more teasing. With a little maneuvering, his brother managed to put them both at the end of the line of parishioners leaving the sanctuary.

"I heard you hanging out with Miss Dawn last night," Blue said.

"Where'd you hear that?" Trip asked, wary. He hadn't thought about the potential for gossip getting around when he'd taken Savannah Dawn up on her invitation.

"Relax, brother. I meant I actually heard the two of you laughing in her cabin while I was on my way home. How late did you stay?"

Trip scowled at Blue. "I left at midnight. We were playing cards. I didn't think we were being that loud."

"I only came close enough to hear because I was hoping to find she had some leftovers of those little meatball boudin things she made. I decided not to come in 'cause I didn't want to cramp your style."

"Oh please," Trip protested. "We're just friends. She's nice."

Blue snorted in disbelief. "Nice is the last word I'd use to describe Miss Dawn," Blue said. "Sensuous, intriguing, heck—sexy is the word."

"Hey, you're married, remember?"

"Oh, I remember all right. Miss Dawn has nothing on my honey, but I do remember your type."

"My type?" Trip repeated. "I don't have a type. Even if I did, there's no one like Miss Dawn in this town. Never has been."

"Uh-huh," Blue agreed with a smile. "And that, dear brother, is your type. Kate was a one-of-a-kind too. At least, we both thought so."

"Kate . . . ," Trip began, then realized his voice was carrying in the rapidly emptying room. He lowered his voice and tried again. "Kate was a selfish heartbreaker who let me believe we wanted the same things out of life before she found her ticket out and left me—" He stopped. Blue already knew most of this, but there were some things almost no one knew about what Kate did before she left.

"She was also a ginger in a town of browns and blondes." Blue held up his hand to forestall any further argument. "All right, you and Miss Dawn are just playing nice. But brother, you maybe ought to check into that. I think—"

They caught sight of a new arrival, causing Blue to shut his trap and Trip to sigh in relief. He wasn't sure he could explain that what drew him to Savannah Dawn wasn't just her looks and mysterious ways, it was her intelligence, her sexy sass, her vulnerability—the whole package.

"Miss Jules," Blue said, putting his fingers to his forehead in greeting. "How are you this fine Sunday?"

"I'm well, Blue. How are Mitzi and the baby?"

"They're good. She's twelve weeks along now, just starting to show."

Jules gave a serene smile, though Trip knew it was a hard question for her to ask since she'd never managed to have kids of her own before her husband died.

Blue was understandably uncomfortable. He mumbled something about finding Mitzi and turned toward the door. Trip just shook his head. His brother could be slow about some things, but at least he had the decency not to spout his theories in front of Jules. He respected her enough not to say anything that might hurt her.

Trip gave Jules an appropriately modest hug and whispered into her ear. "I was going to search you out."

She stepped back from him with another smile that

seemed a little anxious. "Care to sit?" she asked, and motioned to a pew. He was surprised but followed her lead. "What's on your mind?"

Trip rubbed the bridge of his nose for a moment. One of the great things about Jules was he could always talk to her—even more so than his own brother. She had no expectations of him, no claim on him, nothing but a mutual respect and the little matter of their "friends with benefits" arrangement. And that was what made this conversation hard.

"I'm confused as hell, Jules. I don't know if you heard, but Momma found a cook for us out at the ranch and... well . . . ," he tugged his ear, "I want to say she's beautiful. I've never seen someone as pretty as her." He blushed. "Not to say you're not pretty, it's just—"

"It's all right, Trip." Jules gave his hand a pat. "You don't have to worry about my feelings. Does this beauty have a name?"

"Sa—" Trip opened his mouth to say her name but caught himself just in time. "She's Dawn. See, that's another thing. She's got this mysterious thing going on, and I'm just itching to know more about her. We played cards for three hours last night, and I kind of feel like I know her, except I don't know anything *about* her. Does that make sense? She's funny, clever, and sexy as the day is long, but she's also afraid of something." He checked to make sure no one was near enough to hear him. "She told Momma she's running from an abusive relationship but I think there's more to the story than that."

"There usually is," Jules agreed.

Trip slumped back against the pew. "So, you think she's trouble?"

Jules gave his shoulder a push and laughed. "I haven't even met her. All I meant to suggest was even if she's telling you her complete truth, there's still another side to the story. Go carefully. Go slowly. For her sake as well as yours. If it's an abusive relationship, she could be more fragile than she seems. If it's something else, it may be something you'll want to stay away from."

She glanced around the room, then reached out and took Trip's hand, assured that the pew back would block her actions from the last lingering souls at the door. Running one finger lightly along his forefinger, she looked up at him through her lashes.

"I'm just happy you've finally found someone who caught your interest," she said.

He ducked his head to better see her face. He half expected to find tears and felt like a first-class jerk when he saw her eyes shining suspiciously.

"Awww, Jules," he said softly.

"It's all right," she repeated. "It's not what you think. I was coming to find you to see if we could take a rain check on this afternoon. Donald Johansson invited me to lunch."

"DJ? From Garden City?" Jules nodded, and Trip continued. "The widower from Garden City?" He smiled and shook his head. "Well I'll be."

That made Jules laugh again. "Don't go jumping to any conclusions," she said. "It's just lunch."

He caught her hand and squeezed it, then risked running his finger along her jawline. "Aren't we a pair?" he said softly. "Seems like both of us might be ready to move on." He paused for a second, then asked, "How come we never worked?"

"We do, Trip. We did and we do. After Will died, I needed someone to turn to. You needed someone after Kate. Someone who knew the pain in our heart, someone who could meet our physical needs without any strings attached, because strings would have been too much to bear. Someone who would allow us to heal. We have been that someone to each other."

"But how come we couldn't take it to the next level?" he asked, his curiosity piqued. "I know you're a bit older, but really, we would have made sense. Instead, we're both happy for the other when it looks like we're ready to move on."

She smiled, though a single tear slid down her cheek. "I don't question it. I just think it's the beautiful thing about us. About Dawn . . . . Talk to her, show her she can trust you, figure out if your attraction to her is more than physical, then follow your heart. It won't lead you astray."

chapter
eleven

S avannah was surprised to discover she felt nervous as she carried a covered dish of her slightly modified jambalaya up to the gate leading behind the main house.

Maddy had come down to help her with breakfast and invite her to Sunday dinner at the main house. It was a new tradition to have the whole family gather, Maddy had told her, and she had help in the kitchen to prepare a dinner, so all Savannah had to do was attend. Everyone would be there, including the hands.

Savannah had tried to decline, but Maddy insisted she was as good as family already. Rather than arrive empty-handed, she had come with something to share.

Since the weather was fine, they had set two giant trestle tables up on the lawn behind the house. Rounding the corner, Savannah found a kind of organized chaos as well over a dozen people milled around, setting up benches and chairs, bringing platters and dishes out to the tables.

She paused on the edge of the activity, not at all sure where she needed to be. When Trip caught sight of her and waved her over to him, she smiled in relief. Of them all—aside from Maddy—Trip was the one she knew the best. As she closed in on his position, he stepped toward her and relieved her of the pot so he could put it on a third table laden with food. Lots of food. She glanced around at all the faces gathered and thought there might just be enough to feed everyone. She'd never been around people who ate so heartily as the ranch hands yet still managed to be fit and lean—a testament to how hard they worked.

There were a few faces she didn't recognize, notably women. One was the waitress from the café, the one she'd met on her first day in town, but she couldn't remember her name. Another was a blonde woman who could very well be the waitress's mother. Then there was a brunette with a crooked smile who looked up at Blue with a kind of sassy adoration. She had a certain aura about her that made Savannah look at her stomach. Sure enough, there was what looked like a baby bump.

She felt a little lost in the clamor until Trip's hand at the small of her back gently guided her toward the women. When he leaned in to speak close to her ear, she gave an involuntary shiver.

"I don't think you've met all the Thomas women."

Mute, she shook her head, shooting him a glance as they completed their approach.

"Dawn, this here is my sister, Janie, and her daughter, Kylie," he said, indicating the two blonde women. "And this short shot is Mitzi, Blue's wife."

Snapping out of her stupor, she smiled at them, then turned slightly to dig her elbow into Trip's side. "Short! She's taller than I!"

Mitzi laughed and stepped forward to compare. "No, I think you've got an inch or so on me. It's nice to meet you, Dawn. I've been hearing good things about your cooking from my insatiable husband."

"Me too," said Janie. "Tim has been raving about it."

She remembered the wrangler's helper, Tim, and Janie were together—a fairly recent development, she'd been given to understand by the gossip at the chow hall.

"You're very kind to say so, Janie," she said, feeling as though her face was on fire. To cover it, she turned to Kylie. "I remember you from the café, that first day I was in town."

Kylie grinned at her. "Yeah! I'm glad to see you're still here and that things seem to be working out. Jax has had nothing but good to say about your cooking too."

"*Mersi*," she said, feeling overwhelmed at their welcoming words. Before she could think of how to engage in any more small talk, Maddy rang a triangle bell hanging off the porch.

"All right, everyone!" she called out. "You know the drill. Help yourself down the buffet, then grab a chair. Once we're all seated we'll say grace, so if you're hungry, you'll move your butts."

There was a general burst of laughter, but there was also a quick formation into a line that split around both sides of the table. More than one person wanted to know what was in the dish Savannah brought, so she took a moment to explain, then watched as most everyone took a small serving. She wished she'd made more—wished everyone could have a bit bigger share. Then again, she knew how these buffet dinners usually worked. Even when one tried to limit portion sizes, one still ended up with far too much food.

She was surprised and grateful when Trip stayed close as they filled their plates, and even more pleased when he sat down beside her at one of the tables. She was also surprised to see the family members spread out among the ranch hands in a manner that seemed completely random.

Blue and Mitzi sat together, and Jax and Kylie. . . basically each couple stayed together, but they didn't form one table for family and one for employees. It really did feel like one big family.

Once everyone had their food and was seated they linked hands, and Maddy led them in a prayer.

"Dear heavenly Father, we thank You for once again gifting us with a fine day to gather as a family in Your sight. We no longer take our time together for granted, and we honor Your gift by breaking bread together. In Your name, we pray. Amen."

"Amen." The word echoed in murmurs around the table, and Savannah added her own acknowledgement into the mix. She wasn't especially religious, but the heartfelt prayer was one she could appreciate. She could get behind honoring a God who valued love and family.

Then, like a levee breaking, everyone moved to grab their forks and dug into the food heaping their plates. Savannah had not held back in loading her own plate, and she was glad for it. No one was showing the least inhibition about shoveling food into their mouths between snatches of conversation.

As the meal wore on, she caught Mitzi watching her closely from across the table and several seats away. Each time, Mitzi smiled sheepishly, then looked away. After the fourth time, Savannah frowned, wondering what was wrong.

She leaned toward Trip, gratified he was paying close enough attention that he immediately leaned toward her in response. "Do I have something in my teeth?" she asked, keeping her voice to a whisper.

Trip turned his head to give her an appraising look. "Not that I can see," he said. "Why?"

"Mitzi keeps staring at me. I figured something must be

out of place?" She left it as a question rather than a statement.

"No, you look fantastic. She probably . . . ." His voice trailed off, and she raised an eyebrow at him. To her delight, he gave her a rather shy smile. "It's kind of a family mission to see me get a girlfriend. She's probably trying to determine whether you could make the cut."

"I see," she said, nodding. "Is that why you have no woman? Your family is too. . . picky?"

Trip searched her gaze for a moment, then gave her a soulful smile. "I haven't really given them cause to put someone to the test recently."

Before she could question that, he cleared his throat. "I'm going to get some pie. Would you like something, Miss Dawn?"

Trip was running away from the direction the conversation had turned. It was not something he wanted to talk about—not with the potential of everyone hearing it, or worse, chiming in with their own observations—so he was putting a pie between them.

She smiled and nodded. "Yes, pie would be wonderful. Can I get us some coffee to go with it?"

"Great idea."

They each moved to accomplish their own mission. Moments later, they were seated again, two plates and two coffee cups before them.

"Wasn't sure whether you wanted peach or apple, so I got one of each," he said as he settled beside her.

She looked between the two plates and smiled. "Yes."

That made him laugh. "I take it either one works for you?" When she nodded, his smile grew bigger. "How about we cut each slice in half so we both can have some of each?"

"Perfect," she said.

chapter
twelve

Trip tried hard not to feel self-conscious as he and Savannah Dawn moved farther away from the gathering. After they'd finished their pie, he had gone with her when she said she wanted to look at Momma's garden. Now they were just wandering down the rows of strawberry plants, looking for any late fruit. She had brought a basket, and they plucked the ripe berries they found and put them in it.

"Do you have a plan for these?" Their fingers brushed lightly as he passed another berry over.

"Maybe," she said, a sly smile on her lips. He had to drag his gaze away from them and the accompanying thought of kissing them. "Maybe I eat them all myself."

His face must have registered his shock because she laughed, which made him smile. He was pretty sure he had smiled more in the last week than he had in the last year.

"You have a wonderful smile," she said, right out of the blue. "You should smile more." It was almost like she'd read his mind.

"If you stick around, I probably will," he said, not

bothering to filter his response. She obviously hadn't filtered hers.

"You mean to say *I* make you smile?" It was her turn to be shocked.

He shrugged, then stooped to pick another berry—the same one she happened to reach for. Their hands collided, and he let his fingers smooth over the spot where he'd jabbed her.

"Sorry," he said, at the same moment she said, "*Mo chagren.*"

He glanced up to see she looked a little flustered, so he leaned back to give her a bit more space. "Was that Creole?"

"Louisiana Creole, yes," she said, nodding. "*Mo chagren,* it means 'I'm sorry.' I. . . sometimes forget I should speak English. It's silly, no? You'd think I was born in another country."

"I couldn't say whether it's silly or not, but it's sure sexy as hell."

Instead of flustering her more, as he'd expected, his comment brought out another laugh. "With charm like that, Colton Thomas the Third, it truly surprises me you're not married."

He didn't realize how still he'd gotten until she looked up at him in alarm. "What's wrong?"

"I . . . ." He shook his head, feeling his cheeks burn with embarrassment. "Sorry."

"No, Trip. I'm the one who's sorry. I said something to upset you."

He tugged his ear as he looked out over the river in the near distance where clouds of newly-hatched mayflies danced above the water. "It's stupid, really. I feel like an idiot for letting it get to me. It was just something similar to what Kate used to say to me."

"Kate?"

He nodded, not daring to look at Savannah Dawn. "She was. . . well, we were engaged for a while." She was patient while he let the emotions roll through him—emotions he should have been able to let go of by now. When he felt like he could go on, he said, "She hurt me. Broke my heart in three pieces."

"Three?" she asked, and her quiet question caused him to look at her at last. Only one other person—Jules—had ever bothered to ask.

"Yep, three," he said, trying to make his tone light. He almost managed it. Almost. "One for me, one for her, and one for . . . ." He couldn't finish.

That was the real reason he hadn't been able to move on after Kate. It wasn't just that she'd killed their plans for a future together in favor of a modeling career in Los Angeles . . . .

Savannah Dawn didn't ask him to continue. Instead, she set the basket down and took his hand in both of hers. He searched her gaze, looking for signs of pity, but instead he saw a kind of answering pain.

They stood like that for several moments. Just when he began to feel awkward, she squeezed his hand, then let go so she could pick up the basket.

"I think we lose the light soon," she said. "I'd like a few more so I can make something in particular for tomorrow."

"Let me help," he said, eager to put his moment of weakness behind him.

TRIP WOKE SLOWLY from the best sleep he'd had in a long time. He'd gone to bed fairly early, after talking out in the garden with Savannah Dawn until the mosquitoes had driven them indoors. Their conversation hadn't delved back to the depths they'd reached when he'd told her about Kate, but he still felt as though he was getting to know her. At least, the part she let him see.

A glance at the clock told him it was close to dawn. Dawn. Savannah Dawn. A beautiful name for a beautiful woman.

He reached over and turned off his alarm clock, then sat up and rubbed his face. He didn't have his usual desire to watch the sunrise. Not alone anyway.

Swiftly and silently, he pulled on his work clothes, then slipped downstairs to the door. It was cool outside again, a warning of sorts that summer was drawing to a close.

Across the yard, lights were on in the kitchen of the chow hall and he could see Savannah Dawn moving around inside. Above him, the sky was beginning to show signs of light. They were closing in on sunrise. Could he get Scotchie ready so he could give Savannah Dawn a ride to the ridge in time to see it?

Would she want to go? There was a good chance she wouldn't want or be able to go. She had to have food on the table for the hands pretty much right at sunrise so they could eat and start their day on time. If she wasn't ready for that, he would have eight men late for work or starting their day hungry. Neither seemed like a good option.

He sighed and looked skyward again. There were no clouds, nothing that might make this sunrise any more special than a hundred others he'd watched. No, what would make this one special would be seeing it with Savannah Dawn.

Bottom line, he just wasn't selfish enough to steal her away like that. So he could do the next best thing.

Crossing the yard with purpose, he stepped up on the porch, opened the door to the chow hall without knocking, and pushed through the swinging door to the kitchen.

She spun around as he entered, a knife up in a defensive posture. Once she saw it was him, she lowered the knife and gave him a too-brilliant smile, but he didn't miss the way her hand shook. "Trip. You startled me."

"I'm sorry, Miss Dawn." He held his hands up slightly, like a gunslinger trying to reassure an opponent he didn't want to draw. "I thought you would have seen me cross the yard."

"Oh, no. I didn't. I've been a little preoccupied this morning."

"What's going on? Can I help?"

She nodded. "Do you grate cheese? I completely forgot to prepare for this morning, and now I'm behind."

"Show me." All thought he'd had of sneaking her off to see the sunrise, or even just inviting her to a future sunrise, went to the back burner when he saw how distressed she was—how disappointed she was in herself for failing to prepare properly.

Within moments she had set him up with a block of cheese, a grater, and a bowl, and he began to help her make the hands the same omelet she'd made him Saturday night. They didn't talk, other than exchanging food related questions and answers. Trip just let himself enjoy her company and marveled at her skill in the kitchen.

SAVANNAH's initial thrill at having Trip's help for breakfast came to a screeching halt shortly after everyone left and she was alone with him once again.

The night before, she'd left the garden feeling mellow and safe, if fatigued from the effort of socializing with so many people at once.

Despite being out of practice, she'd found it easy to slip back into the flirty persona that had always been required of her at social functions. Though, remembering her cover story in front of so many new faces had been a challenge to her fledgling efforts as a liar.

Doubtless it was that combination of old and new skills which had triggered the nightmares that had plagued her all night. She'd tossed and turned with images of poor Dion's terrified face, followed by jabs of remorse as her brain supplied imaginings of the decimation left behind when she'd cut and ran. Who else had suffered for her decisions? How many more people had she exposed to danger?

She'd finally shut down out of sheer exhaustion when the crisp air of early morning cooled her fevered dreams.

Trip had been her savior after she'd woken late to a new sense of panic—she hadn't done any prep for the morning meal. With his help, though, she'd gotten back on track.

When he offered to help with the dishes, she hadn't turned him away.

But now he was standing beside her, drying while she washed. The question he'd asked was still burning in her ears, but she couldn't make herself answer. She continued scrubbing as though she hadn't heard him, hoping he'd take the hint as he'd done before. Instead, he sighed.

"Look, Miss Dawn, I know you're scared and think you can't tell me, but I can handle whatever it is. If I know, we can figure out how to keep you safe. It's just. . . you fit in here. You could have a home here, if you want it."

She turned to stare at him, and he faltered to a stop, his eyes searching her gaze. She didn't know where he was headed with this. What did he mean "have a home here"? What did he think was happening between them?

And could she continue to deny her own feelings if he persisted?

"You wanna leave it alone," she said in warning, as much to herself as him.

"Fine," he said at last. He tossed the dish towel onto the counter before turning and pushing his way through to the chow hall. The thumping of his cowboy boots faded into the distance as he walked away, and she closed her eyes.

"It doesn't matter," she said to the empty room. "I'll never be safe again." The words she'd been telling herself for months now felt hollow, as though maybe something had changed with her arrival here.

Maybe she could learn to trust the Thomas family. Trust Trip. He had been so attentive and patient, always the perfect gentleman despite the attraction that crackled between them. More than once, he'd made her forget the danger she was in, made her feel like she had a friend for the first time in a very long time.

That meant he was either her greatest hope. . . or the greatest risk to the freedom she'd run so far to find.

Resolutely, she returned to the task of cleaning up, hoping the work would provide answers. . . or at least a distraction from the churning confusion threatening to drown her.

One thing was clear: she owed Trip an apology.

T rip found himself drawn to the sound of singing coming from the chow hall kitchen. He had told himself he would stay away from Savannah today. Stay away from the confusion she caused in him, his desire to help and her refusal to allow him to get close.

But the singing drew him in like a bee to a flower. Esmeralda used to sing while she worked, and so did his mother, but they had never sung like that. The tune was sweet yet saucy, and the Creole words he could understand —words similar to the French he'd learned in school—told him the song was about love.

Despite the sound of his boot heels on the porch, the singing didn't stop. He paused in the doorway and watched Savannah chop fruit into chunks for a fruit salad. She swayed her hips in a way that made him take note of her curves. Once again, he was surprised at how her presence reached out to fill the room. Even the hairs on his arms stood out at the sight of her, as if to pull him toward her.

It was a moment before he realized she knew he was there and didn't care if he heard her song. She stopped chopping long enough to wave him closer, and he couldn't have kept his distance if he'd tried. Her song ended, and she tilted her head to look up at him, watching him beneath lowered lashes. He could still make out the hazel-green of those bedroom eyes and felt a shiver as he moved into the room. It was all he could do to put the cooking island between them to keep him from taking her into his arms and kissing her senseless. Except he was pretty sure he'd be the one who would end up senseless.

"Savannah," he breathed. Not quite the greeting he had aimed for. It was a moment before he realized he'd used her real name.

"Hello, *shær*," she said, her voice seductive and smooth, her accent stronger than he'd ever heard it. "Do you like my little song?"

"Yes," he said. "What does it mean?"

She laughed—a deep, throaty chuckle. "Just a little voodoo magic to draw you in, *shær*. I called, and you came." She winked at him as though she was joking, but Trip could have sworn it was the truth.

He cleared his throat. "Now that you have me, what can I do for you?"

She set the knife on the cutting board and lifted a cantaloupe from the basket. He watched in fascination as she held it in both hands, turning it, squeezing it, weighing it. "The fruit, it is hard to get in this part of the country, yes?"

He blinked and dragged his gaze away from her hands, once again looking into her eyes. "Melons, yes. The season is short, and we can extend it only so far with greenhouses. Most of the year we have to get them from the store, and the store doesn't always get the best produce."

"But this melon is from the farm here, non? It is *byin*, good. I was hoping to make fruit salad for the men, but I'm afraid there's not enough."

"I reckon the men won't notice. They're not much on fruits anyway."

"Why not?" Her voice expressed complete surprise. "Fruit is good."

Trip shrugged. "No protein, empty calories."

"*Mé non!* It's good. Natural sugar, carbohydrates for energy, great tastes. It's like eating love."

"I'm sorry. Eating love?"

"*Wi.* Fruit is sexy."

Trip laughed. "Sexy? I don't think so."

"You never take a bite of strawberry and feel the rush of passion?"

"No," he said with another laugh.

"Try," Savannah said, reaching into the basket and pulling out a ripe, red strawberry. She cut it in half and handed it to him. "*Manjé.* Eat."

"I don't think—"

"Eat." She gestured to her mouth, urging him by example.

"All right," he said, then popped the berry into his mouth. He chewed and swallowed in one bite. "So?"

"Not like that!" she scolded. "Come. Try again."

"I don't—"

She held up a hand to stop him. His eyes followed her as she moved around the counter with slow deliberation, not stopping until she was well within his personal space. Catching his gaze with hers, she brought the other half of the berry up to his lips, tracing it lightly along the edges.

"Eat," she whispered.

Holding her gaze, he opened his mouth. She teased the berry in then away when he tried to bite. She smiled, leaning into him with her hip. She pressed again, then let him bite just the end. The difference in the experience was. . . sensational. From the sweet flavor on his tongue to the crisp feel of the berry's flesh breaking between his teeth. As dumb as his mind thought he was being, he felt his body react to the experience.

"Oh," he sighed. "I see."

"Do you?" She reached into the bowl to bring up a chunk of cantaloupe.

Her gaze moved until she stared at his lips, tracing the juicy piece against them as she'd done with the berry. He flicked his tongue out to taste, and its sweetness felt like fire. She teased it away, then brought it close again. He bit into it before she could pull it back.

Without realizing she had moved, he felt her free hand at the base of his neck, drawing him down so she could bite the rest of the melon. Her lips met his in a kiss that was an explosion of taste and sensation and a rushing of life into his body. Even after the melon was gone, he tasted her, moving his lips over hers as though he could devour her. Their tongues entwined, a promise of more sweet sensations to come.

Wrapping his hands around her waist, he pulled her against him, and she melded with him, her fingers sliding over the short hair at the nape of his neck to hold him close. He wanted her even closer.

This. This was a woman who might be able to fill the chasm Kate had left behind. He felt truly alive for the first time in years.

Then Savannah Dawn pulled away, moving back around the counter as though nothing had happened. As though she kissed men that way every day.

"I told you," she said with a smile. "Sexy, *non?*"

Trip drew in a ragged breath, trying to regain his bearings. "Didn't you . . . ?" he began, then cleared his throat and tried again. "Didn't you *feel* that?"

"*Mé wé*. But of course," she said happily. "That is the

why. I love to feel the food I eat. You can see this, non?" She ran her hands down her sides from her breasts to her hips, outlining her luscious curves and stealing his breath away yet again. "Maybe too much love?"

He shook his head slowly, still trying to regroup. "That was . . . . You are. . . perfect."

She tilted her head at him and winked as she picked up the knife and cut another melon in half. "*Mersi*. Now, you had something you came to say to me?"

The question sent Trip's mind racing as he tried to remember why he had come into the kitchen in the first place. All he could think of was her singing and that kiss. He licked his lips again, still tasting more than the melon's sweetness.

Savannah gave him a knowing smile and returned to chopping the fruit, humming the song she had been singing when he came in.

Voodoo magic. No one could convince him it wasn't real now. He would never again look at fruit the same way.

SAVANNAH DIDN'T FEEL NEARLY as calm as she pretended to be. She kept chopping melon into chunks, knowing she had just brazenly kissed her boss and apparently knocked him for a loop the same way she had surprised herself.

It had been totally spur of the moment and easily one of the most erotic kisses she'd ever shared with a man. She'd been speaking the truth. She definitely found food to be sexy, but she hadn't expected the explosion of taste and sensation kissing him had triggered.

She didn't know what had come over her. One minute she'd been giving him her "food is sexy" speech, then she'd acted, trying to steal away the bite of melon she'd just fed him.

If she'd expected anything, it might have been a laugh at the silly antic, or maybe even revulsion at sharing food in such a way, but she'd felt a deep stab of passion that had turned her on more than any kiss ever had.

Now he was staring at her as she worked, and she was trying to play it cool when she felt anything but.

"I came by," he began, then cleared his throat and started again. "I came by to apologize for pushing you this morning. I upset you, and that wasn't my goal. I—"

"It's fine," she said quickly, not wanting him to feel like he'd been in the wrong. "You just want to help, I know this. I overreacted. If anything, I owe you an apology."

Trip shook his head. "I want you to feel safe here, that's all. You are safe, whether you tell me your problem or not. I want . . . ." He paused as if searching for the right words, then threw up his hands in surrender. "I want to be your friend."

Savannah set the knife down and looked at him across the island counter. She wanted to cross to him and take his face in her hands, kiss that worried look away, but she held her ground. It would be the worst thing she could do in this situation. She needed the safety she knew she could find out here. She couldn't chance ruining it by escalating a mutual crush into some kind of fling they would both regret.

"You are my friend," she said at last.

They stared at each other for long moments, and she wished she could read his mind.

Finally, he nodded. "Good." Then he turned on his heel and left.

It was another few moments before she began chopping fruit again.

DEPUTY MITZI THOMAS sat back in her chair, her left hand reflexively flattening on the growing bulge of her belly.

"Well hell," she said, causing Deputy Quince to look across the desk at her.

"Anything I should know about?" he asked, and she shook her head.

"Not sure." That was a lie.

It was Monday morning, and she'd come into the Sheriff's office early because a nagging notion had kept her from sleep. She'd seen Dawn Saint-Aime somewhere before. It had only been a slight tug after the first Sunday lunch, one she'd been able to dismiss, but something she'd seen in the woman's demeanor her second time joining the family lunch had struck a memory.

She'd tried to ask Maddy about the woman, but her mother-in-law was uncharacteristically quiet on the matter. She tried to convince herself there was nothing to know about the beautiful woman, who by all accounts had blown into the truck stop for some coffee and a cup of soup and ended up cooking for the hands out at the Lazy J.

There had been nothing about the story that had raised any red flags for Mitzi before the first dinner she'd attended. She'd been pleased to hear the Lazy J had finally found a cook. It took the pressure off her to provide meals for her husband. She had never picked up the knack for cooking more than her few specialty items, and Blue, though he'd never say anything, had been less than enthusiastic about mealtimes—until the new cook had arrived.

This Sunday was the second time she'd seen the beauty who looked like a cover model for Ebony. When Sheriff Jonas had shown up unexpectedly to ask her a question, it had seemed Dawn couldn't get out of his sight fast enough. She'd practically tripped over a bench to get inside.

Mitzi couldn't get it out of her head that she'd been trying to hide something. And that had re-triggered the notion that she'd seen her before.

After all, how could anyone forget such a face?

In Denver, she may have gone unnoticed in all the information sheets that crossed across her desk, but in Hamilton County, Kansas?

No. Raven-black hair, skin the color of wheat in a warm field, stunning hazel eyes, not to mention the exotic accent—a one in a million visitor. A one in a million bulletin.

That was the thought that had prompted her to look through the various bulletins from the last several months.

When she found the flyer, she thought maybe it had been a mistake, a missing persons filed with the "Be on the Lookout" bulletins, but when she went to double check it . . . .

Mitzi stared at the screen, still wondering if it was some kind of mistake. But there it was, Dawn's face on the national BOLO listing. Only . . . .

"Be on the lookout for Savannah Montault De Saint-Cirié of New Orleans, Louisiana. Wanted as a person of interest in a crime. Considered a high flight risk. Do not engage. Notify FBI in New Orleans and await instructions."

The photo, a surveillance picture obviously taken without the subject's consent, showed a woman on the run. She looked hunted, terrified, as she looked up, apparently catching sight of the security camera.

Mitzi knew that feeling all too well.

On a hunch, she swapped over to a search engine and

typed in the woman's last name. A name like Montault De Saint-Cirié would bring up focused results.

Surprisingly, the top hits were about some politician in New Orleans. Nothing scandalous, nothing untoward. An old family name, old money, outgoing Mayor of New Orleans, now on track for a run at Governor of Louisiana. Obviously whatever this Savannah had done or was involved in, it wasn't tied to a public scandal.

Mitzi sat back again, rubbing her belly absently. Something didn't feel right. It was the look in Savannah's eyes as she'd been photographed. That expression didn't fit the profile of a criminal on the run.

But she was walking on dangerous ground here. If it got out that she'd seen the subject of a BOLO and didn't report it, especially someone categorized as a flight risk, it could mean suspension from her job. On the other hand, she knew what it meant to be hunted like that. She was torn, wondering if she should offer a sympathetic ear instead of calling it in.

"You look like someone just kicked your dog," Quince said. Mitzi looked up to see him holding out a file folder.

"Hmmm? Sorry. Just lost in thought. What's that?"

Quince leaned forward, and Mitzi resisted the urge to flip the Google search away. "It's the boss's birthday card, remember?" He raised his eyebrows. "The one you started passing around Friday morning?"

"Oh yeah, right," she stammered. "Sorry. I swear, these pregnancy hormones have ruined my memory."

Quince smiled and leaned back. "No worries. My wife was the same way."

Mitzi smiled as he went back to his desk, then flipped back to stare at the photo in the BOLO file and wondered what to do.

chapter
fourteen

The ping of a notification drew Laurencett's attention to the popup in the corner of his monitor. He stopped typing the email he'd been composing to take a closer look, then clicked on the box to open the dialog window.

"It's about time," he muttered, then reached for his phone. Dialing out, he waited for the line to connect then spoke before the person on the other end had a chance to say anything. "I need a meeting. I'll be there in half an hour."

He hung up, clicking open a few more windows to chain through several pages of data, skimming the content before sending the information to his phone. He could study up on the cab ride over.

Exactly thirty minutes later the butler escorted him into Mama Sanci's office, and he stood waiting for her to acknowledge him. When she looked up, he gave her a tight smile.

"Where?" Mama asked, immediately discerning the nature of the news he had to deliver in person—the kind of news that could never be discussed on an open phone line.

"Western Kansas. A deputy sheriff in Hamilton County pinged her BOLO today. Followed up with a Google search. It's not a guaranteed strike, but I'm confident enough to put out word. I've got people who can be out there in short order. If she's there, we'll find her."

Mama Sanci smiled, and Laurencett was glad she wasn't smiling like that about a *mistake* he'd made.

"Excellent."

SAVANNAH CHECKED out the window again. This time, she saw Scotchie standing at the porch rail and Trip dismounting by the light of the halide lamps in the yard.

A surge of excitement coursed through her. To quell it, she checked to make sure everything was in order.

A sheet pan heaped with split bagels was covered on the countertop, and a tray of sliced meats, cheese, and spreads was ready in the refrigerator. Two insulated carafes were filled with coffee and another pot was prepped and ready to brew, needing only a press of the button to start. There was also a small assortment of cold cereals and some hard-boiled eggs.

It was by no means a special meal, but Trip had assured her it would not be the first time the ranch hands had needed to resort to a simple breakfast. There was no other way to do what he'd invited her to do: finally watch a sunrise with him. They had enlisted Jax's help. The young man had been informed where everything was, and he was to make sure it all made it to the table.

Trip appeared in the doorway, searching out her worried gaze.

"Are you sure this is all right?" she asked.

He smiled. "One of the perks of being a Thomas on the Lazy J. C'mon. The sunrise waits for no one. It'll be cool up there on the rise." He held out her jacket and helped her into it when she crossed the room.

She took a deep breath and followed him out onto the porch. He brought Scotchie close to the steps so she could mount up.

"It's been a decade since I've ridden," she said, pausing as she fitted her shoe into the stirrup. White sneakers were the most suitable footwear she had to go riding in, and she knew from experience that they wouldn't stay white long if she wore them riding often. Wouldn't stay white long just being out here on the ranch. She shook her head and swung her leg over Scotchie's back so she could settle into the saddle. She wasn't going to be here that long. Was she?

"I'd never have known," he said, and she felt herself blushing at the compliment. Her cheeks heated even more as he swung up behind her with the ease and grace of someone who rode every day.

It had been a week and a day since she'd kissed him in her kitchen. A week of semi-awkward meetings around the ranch where they'd both tried to play it cool amid the heat of an attraction she was sure was mutual. He'd started eating nearly all his meals at the chow hall and had taken some ribbing from the rest of the hands, who seemed oblivious to anything other than the food being the reason.

She got the sense he didn't usually spend so much time near the main house, judging by some of the remarks from Blue and Maddy, and even his sister, Janie—when she was there. But if any of his behavior was truly remarkable, no one was saying anything, and she was glad.

Now, as he scooted in close to her and wrapped one arm around her waist while the other gathered the reins, she caught her breath. Maybe this wasn't the smartest idea. She'd been trying to maintain some kind of distance, but there was no such thing as distance in what they were doing now.

His head leaned over her shoulder as he clicked his tongue to urge the horse forward, and she suppressed a shiver at the proximity of his mouth to her ear.

"Are you cold?" he asked.

Unable to speak, she shook her head. His chuckle said he knew exactly what had triggered that response, and his left arm snugged a bit more firmly around her waist.

"It's getting cooler in the mornings," he said conversationally as they made their way up the hill of the driveway. "Won't be long before we have a frost."

Savannah found herself leaning back against him as they began to climb the hill in earnest. She chuckled to herself. "Frost! That's not something I know much about. I can count on one hand the number of times we've had frost at home."

"And frost is just the start. Winter up here means snow on the ground for months. Do you think that's something you'll be able to deal with?"

"I won't know until I try. It'll certainly be different."

She kept her eyes straight ahead, trying to see into the inky darkness now that they were away from the lights of the compound. It was a little eerie, and she was glad for Trip's company. As if sensing her discomfort, his arm tightened around her middle.

They rode in silence for a few minutes, then she felt a subtle change. The ground leveled out as they reached the top of the hill. Shapes of what might have been trees materialized into view around her. She remembered the trees she could see at the top of the hill from below, and these shadows helped her orient herself. Then Scotchie stopped, and Trip urged him to turn around, where she could see a definite brightening in the sky.

She hugged her arms around herself as a breeze that had been behind them now blew into her face, making her cold.

Trip wrapped both his arms around her, his coat open to include her in its warmth, and leaned his head on her shoulder so some of the wind was blocked.

"Better?" he asked.

She nodded, unable to speak once again.

The sky grew lighter. She made out wisping shreds of fog lifting from the prairie as the lights of the stars began going out in greater numbers. She could almost imagine a pop as the leading edge of the sun cleared the horizon. Fluffy little clouds caught fire in the rays of the sun, dazzling her with brightness.

"It's lovely," she told Trip, and pressed her cheek against his hard enough to feel the stubble of his morning beard.

"Yes, you are," he said, and she realized he hadn't been paying attention to nature's sideshow.

She turned her head to look at him. Their proximity was too tempting. Snaking one hand up between herself and his arm, she touched his cheek, then leaned in to kiss him.

It was an awkward kiss, over her shoulder, but it was still tender and left her feeling as though nothing in the world existed besides them.

TRIP HELD himself still as his lips met Savannah Dawn's. The moment was precious and perfect, and he didn't want to do anything to mess it up. It wasn't meant to be a long kiss. She hadn't closed her eyes, and he didn't want to miss anything so he'd kept his open too. The electricity that had been building between them sparked, holding them together a few heartbeats longer.

Savannah's eyes fluttered closed, and he squeezed her a little tighter. Apparently he tightened his leg muscles too, enough to give Scotchie mixed messages. The gelding took a step forward, which caused Savannah to clutch at him in surprise as she leaned back.

"Easy," he said, forcing himself to relax.

"Are you talking to me or the horse?" she asked, then chuckled as she nestled against his chest and turned to look to the east again.

"The horse," he said with a laugh. "And maybe myself. I gotta tell you, Miss Dawn, kissing you has been on my mind a lot. I worried you would think this was a total setup to get you alone so I could stage another kiss."

"Was it not a setup?" There was a note of humor in her voice that told him whatever his answer, it would be okay.

"Yes. I mean, no." He shook his head and chuckled. "I mean, I wanted to share my favorite moment of the day with you, and I guess I hoped you'd respond just the way you did."

Her hand closed around his forearm as she shifted slightly in the saddle, turning so she could rest her cheek against his chest.

"Oh, Trip. What am I going to do about you?" she asked, her voice so soft he wasn't at all sure he was supposed to have heard.

The crunch of tires on gravel caused them both to turn

and look behind them. Savannah's entire body tensed at the sight of a pickup truck headed their way. He recognized the vehicle by the light bar across the top of the cab.

"It's Mitzi," he said, trying to reassure Savannah Dawn, but she didn't relax.

"She's police?" There was a note of panic in her voice.

"County Deputy Sheriff. Why? What's wrong?"

"Oh, no, no, no!" She was struggling to dismount, and her tension made Scotchie skip forward a few steps.

"Miss Dawn, you need to calm down or Scotchie is going to bolt. Do you hear me?" It was a bit of an exaggeration. Scotchie was well-trained, but even he could misbehave when faced with a panicked rider, and Trip wasn't properly in the saddle to control him.

Savannah stopped herself with both legs on one side, ready to slide down, her eyes wide as she stared at the woman exiting the vehicle.

"Good morning," his sister-in-law said. "I've been meaning to talk to you, Savannah."

Trip was pretty sure Mitzi had only been told Savannah Dawn's alias. He frowned now as Mitzi stopped, her hand resting lightly on her sidearm. He had never seen her in full-on cop mode.

"What's going on?" Trip asked.

"Maybe that's something Miss Savannah Montault de Saint-Cirié can tell us both."

chapter
fifteen

Heart pounding, Savannah stared down at the deputy with a kind of fatalistic horror.

Everything was ruined. Everything. If Mitzi knew her real name, that meant she'd been found out, and chances were good Laurencett wouldn't be far behind. She had to make her excuses and get away.

Mitzi frowned into the rising sun and came around the front of the vehicle so she could get a better angle on her. "If you run," she said, her voice neutral, "I'll have no choice but to bring you in."

"What the hell, Mitzi?" Trip asked, his grip around her waist tightening as if he was ready to protect her. She was grateful for that.

Mitzi never broke eye contact with her. "I'm inclined to think there's more to the story than what I read on the data sheet, Savannah," she said, her voice still soothing and level. "But you've got to talk to me. I've been doing my homework, and so far I haven't found any records beyond the BOLO that says you're a person of interest in a crime. What can you tell me about your situation?"

Savannah glanced at Trip, the idea of telling the truth tightening her throat so badly, she didn't think she'd be able to speak even if she thought it was a good idea. How could she, when the truth was just as dangerous to them as it was to her?

Best case scenario, Laurencett's contacts would make sure she came out looking like a criminal. Worse case. . . for all she knew, he would come in here and clean house. She wouldn't put it past him.

"I can see you're frightened," Mitzi continued. "I've been there, not knowing who to trust. Maybe we should all go down to the house, have some coffee, and you can tell me your side of the story."

"My side?" Savannah could hardly believe that was a viable option. It couldn't be safe, could it? But she needed to buy some time. She managed a jerky nod, which Mitzi returned.

"Trip."

Savannah watched the two of them exchange a glance that seemed to say more than words, then Trip urged her to face forward in the saddle again.

"It's going to be all right," Trip said. "Mitzi is a good cop. She'll make sure you're taken care of. And I'll be right next to you while we figure this out, okay?"

All she could do was nod again. Her mind calculated moves a million miles an hour, trying to decide what story she could tell to buy herself enough time to get back on the road and put all the distance she could between here and where she was going.

Her heart sank as she realized the depth of this discovery, how badly she was screwed. She had thought if she went far enough west, they wouldn't think to look for her. She was a Southern girl. They would have expected her to stay in the South, close to what she knew. She'd been banking on that as she'd headed for Bellingham, Washington. If she'd been sighted this far west, they'd surely realize how committed she was to getting away. Crossing into Canada was out of the question now.

Unless maybe she could head due north to some no-name border crossing in Montana. Or sneak across. It wasn't like Canada had a wall.

"Savannah?" Trip's voice was in her ear again, his arms snug around her as he turned Scotchie back toward the compound. "Can you tell me what's going on? What crime?"

She shook her head, even as the words came unbidden to her lips. "Someone is dead because of me."

Trip didn't say anything, didn't ask any more questions, but he did give her a reassuring squeeze. They rode back down the hill toward the barn, Mitzi's patrol truck following at a respectful distance.

Down in the hollow there was still no direct sunlight, but it was light enough to see the buildings as they approached. Trip rode right up to the hitching post near the gate to the front lawn of the main house. Before she could do anything, he was down below her, arms raised to catch her as she slid out of the saddle.

He held her gaze as he put her on her feet, but she couldn't read what he was thinking. Still undecided if she could or should tell him the truth, she squeezed his forearms then let go. They turned together to head up to the house as Mitzi parked the truck and followed them in.

Maddy and Mr. Thomas were still in the dining room having breakfast when they came in. Mr. Thomas looked up, then behind them as he took in the company his son was keeping.

"Good morning, y'all," Maddy said, her cheerful voice faltering when she realized Mitzi was in uniform. "To what do we owe the pleasure?"

"Might turn out to be less than a pleasure," Mitzi said. "May we sit? Savannah has some things she needs to tell us."

"Of course. Sit." Maddy's gaze shifted between the three of them, then flicked to her husband. "Can I get everyone some coffee?"

Savannah felt adrenaline rushing through her, but she nodded, hoping to gain a little more time. Trip went with his mother to get more cups while she and Mitzi pulled out chairs. She stared at her hands, trying to come up with a plausible story that would fit in with what she'd already told them and what may or may not have been on the BOLO.

She could feel Mr. Thomas's eyes on her. Mitzi's too. Neither seemed to be holding any judgment against her— yet—as they waited patiently for the others to return. It didn't take long before Trip handed her a mug of black coffee and Maddy handed one to Mitzi.

Everyone stared at her, and an awkward silence ensued.

Finally, Mitzi cleared her throat and gave Maddy an apologetic look. "I had a feeling I'd seen 'Dawn' some- where before, so I looked into it. I found an information sheet suggesting she's wanted as a person of interest in a crime down in New Orleans. Now, this doesn't say she's guilty of anything, but they do call her a flight risk. I was supposed to call in her whereabouts to the FBI in New Orleans, but after debating with myself all night, I decided I wanted to talk to her first."

It was strange to have Mitzi speaking as though she wasn't even in the room, but it felt in tune with the discon-

nect she felt at being called out like this. She was grateful
Mitzi hadn't called it in or hauled her into the sheriff's
office to sort things out there, but *bondjé*!

"I thought you said you were hiding from your abusive
husband," Maddy said, nothing in her expression except
confused concern.

"You're still married?" Trip asked, then blushed.

Mr. Thomas didn't move, just continued to stare
at her.

She opened her mouth, then closed it and fiddled with
her coffee mug for a moment. "I don't know where to
start," she said at last.

TRIP WATCHED Savannah Dawn struggle to find the words
that would tell them what was going on. He wanted to
help, wanted to tell her it was fine, whatever was going on
could be worked out, but he realized he'd better not inter-
fere. She'd said someone was dead. This was serious.

"Would it be easier if I asked some questions to help
you get started?" Mitzi asked, her tone concerned but not
warm. Professional.

A look of pure panic crossed Savannah's face, but she
gave another jerky nod.

"Okay. Let's start easy. Is your real name Savannah
Montault de Saint-Cirié?"

"*Wi.*"

"And you're from New Orleans?"

"*Wi.*"

"Are you any relation to Mayor Michelle Montault De
Saint-Cirié, the woman who is running for state governor
in November's election?"

"She's my mother." Her answer was little more than a whisper.

"And your husband is . . . ?"

"I have no husband." Her gaze moved to his mother, who frowned. "I'm sorry I lied, but I've had to lie for so long, I feel sometimes I no longer know how to tell the truth." She drew in a deep breath. "I am not married, and there is no abusive husband. I told you so you would let me in, so you would help me."

"I'm sure you had a good reason, Savannah," Momma said. "I just hope you know you can tell us the truth now. We can help you, whatever it is."

Trip glanced again at his father, who had narrowed his eyes as he gazed at Savannah. Momma had a gentle, open heart, willing to see the good in everyone. Daddy was a different story. Daddy had seen enough of the most awful aspects of humanity, he didn't have that automatic trust like Momma did.

"Unless you broke the law." Daddy's gruff voice rumbled into the room for the first time since they'd all sat down. "We don't abide folks who live by their own rules."

Momma laid a gentling hand on Daddy's forearm and he glanced at her, his expression closed.

"I promise you, I didn't break any laws, except maybe speeding. Certainly not any law that would get me in trouble with the FBI. I was just . . . . I tried to do the right thing, but it all came to grief."

Leaning forward, Savannah spoke directly to Trip even though she should have really been talking to Mitzi. She seemed to have come to a decision.

"I'm from New Orleans, as I told you. My family is one of the oldest in the Garden District. There have been Montault de Saint-Ciriés involved in politics for nearly two hundred years. My family is very traditional Creole, and I was raised to speak Louisiana Creole as a first language in my home. I didn't learn English until I was eight, and even then it was not as my primary language. I was schooled in our home until I reached the sixth grade, by a tutor who taught me in Creole first, then English."

She glanced around at her audience. "I tell you this because it is important for you to understand. I have not led an ordinary life. My *popa*, my father, spoiled his only child, and I realized much later how I'd been sheltered from the harsh realities of this world. As a member of the City Council of New Orleans, my *popa* was beloved, a true man of the people. I was sixteen when he died during Hurricane Katrina. He wouldn't evacuate, you see, and died trying to save people from drowning in the floods. He was a good man. My *moman*, my mother, on the other hand . . . ," Savannah paused, her throat working as she swallowed.

"*Moman's* people have also had their fingers in politics since back in the early days, but never elected positions, if you take my meaning. I never heard too much about it directly from them. It was all things I investigated after I met Dion—after things he said reminded me of fights I'd overheard, looks *Moman* would give *Popa* when he couldn't see. I was reminded of a lesson my tutor gave me about families controlling corrupt politicians in New Orleans, and then *Moman* fired him immediately after I'd shared the story with her. I was too naive to know he'd been telling me about *Moman's* family . . . .

"When *Popa* died a hero, *Moman* leveraged his death to get elected, first to his position on the City Council, then to the Mayor's office. As the *shè fiy*, beloved daughter of a hero, she used me to help cultivate her image. I, the sweet innocent deprived of a father, she the grieving widow, fired up and hell bent on fixing the system that failed her husband. And *mo Djé édé*, God help me, I helped her. Like the frog who stays in water slowly coming to a boil, I thought I was doing the right thing. But I eventually began to feel the heat."

She paused again, licked her lips, then took a drink of her cooling coffee. No one spoke, and she closed her eyes before continuing.

"A year ago, there was a political function. *Moman* had just announced her candidacy for governor and she was courting contributions. I, the dutiful daughter, played my part. I made a dish so *Moman* could make a fuss about me, and as I sat alone after, a man approached me, told me his name was Dion and he was an inner-city activist. He engaged me in conversation, and it wasn't until later I learned he had an agenda. I agreed to meet him again, and we became friends of sorts. Then he began to open my eyes about what *Moman* was really doing.

"*Bondjé*, this is a long tale. Let me just give you the shortest version and tell you, my mother, she's a corrupt woman. She makes the former mayor who's now in jail for corruption look like a saint. Diverting federal money to private projects, embezzling money from public funds, using police as her personal enforcers, awarding reconstruction jobs to favored contractors who overbid their work then underperform the quality. You name it, if it makes her money, she is involved.

"I was *malad*, horrified, by the things he told me, of the people who suffer because she tampers with the funding for their social services programs. People who are hurt or killed due to substandard workmanship in housing projects. Small businesses unable to recover because of the fees for forced 'reconstruction associations.'"

She took another drink of coffee, then licked her lips before continuing.

"A few months later, Dion and I went on an outing on *Moman's* sailboat, *Régalé*. He asked me to confront her, threaten to go on record against her. God help me, I said I would."

chapter
sixteen

S avannah couldn't believe she was telling the truth. At least so far. Now she was getting to the truly dangerous part, but she wasn't sure she could stop. It was such a tremendous relief to finally tell her story.

Her mind took her back to the day Dion died.

"We thought we planned our approach carefully. We would ask her to change her ways, be more reflective of my father's values. We hoped to encourage it without forcing a big scandal. She was campaigning, so we knew she wouldn't want any bad press. We thought she would listen . . . ."

The evening light is just beginning to fail in the garden as Dion and I enter the parlor. We chose the hour as the most likely time for Moman to be in a good mood, her meal digested and the stress of her workday set aside for the night.

The household butler, Albert, ghosts past us, turning on a few lamps to supplement the single lamp by Moman's settee, then he stands at attention on her left, ready for the least instruction. As usual, there are no chairs directly facing her.

When Moman looks up from her evening newspaper and sees me, she snaps her fingers. Albert steps forward, moves a single chair so it faces her, then gestures for me to sit. They both effectively ignore Dion's existence.

"What's this, child? Why have you brought this. . . young man to me?"

She skirts a comment on the fact that Dion's skin is too dark to be our kind of Creole. In her messed-up, Colorist hierarchy, if you're not Creole, you're as good as dirt. I had warned Dion of this, and we follow our plan to ignore it if she brings it up. There are bigger concerns at hand.

"Moman, this is Dion. We want to talk to you—"

"I know who he is. He's a troublemaker. He fills people's heads with nonsense and stirs up shyé in the pot. I ask why you bring him to me."

I take a steadying breath. We're off on a bad foot. The prudent thing would be to leave and try another day, ensure she's balanced and not in the midst of one of her diabetic mood swings, but I am too invested in Dion's time-line to think straight.

"I have a proposition for you."

Moman waves her hand dismissively. "I don't need to make deals with my own daughter. There's nothing you have that I want."

Just like that, she dismisses me, and her disdain for me hardens my resolve. "What about my good will?" I ask. "What if I go to the press, tell them I no longer support you? I can do an interview, make a speech—"

"Stop this at once!" she says. Though her voice is hard, I haven't impressed her with my threats.

"No, Moman. I will not lie down. Not anymore. Dion has opened my eyes to the way you treat me, no better than you treat Albert. Since Popa died, I've been nothing more than an asset to you, currency you can leverage to help you win elections. He's shown me the truth about what you do, how you rape this city and leave our citizens bleeding in the gutters—"

I squeak as Moman thrusts herself to her feet and crosses the space between us in two furious steps. Her hand shoots out and cracks across my cheek, snapping my head to one side.

"Do not preach at me, daughter. I will not have it." There is no protestation of innocence, no justification, no plea for understanding. Moman reminds me she is a hard woman who does what she pleases, follows her own rules, and to hell with anyone who tries to stop her.

Dion steps forward to catch her hand when she tries to slap me again. "Mama Sanci," he says, addressing her by the nickname her adoring, blind constituents have given her. "You owe it to Savannah to at least hear her out."

"Owe her? Owe her?" Moman's face mottles red with fury. She shakes her hand free of him. "The only thing I owe her is a whipping for daring to talk back to me. And another for disobeying my wishes by speaking to a darkie like you in the first place. And you! If you ever lay a hand on me, I will—no!"

She spins away from us, perhaps re-thinking this outburst. I have never seen her get so enraged so quickly. I always knew she had a temper, have felt the brunt of it many times, but this demonstration is extreme.

And she's not done. When she turns back to Dion, there's something in her hand I hadn't seen her pick up.

"Albert, hold him," she says. I freeze in my chair as Albert moves up behind Dion and puts an arm lock on him. Albert is a giant of a man who always reminds me of Jim from Huck Finn's raft. Dion can scarcely budge him as he struggles against the hold.

Moman advances on Dion, a look in her eye I will never forget as long as I live. Ice cold and heartless.

"What my husband never understood," she says, "is the fastest way to cure dissent is to mercilessly eliminate it. I will not accept your insolence."

The object she holds is a syringe. Dion's eyes widen with terror, and his mouth forms a small "o." With a flash of clarity, I realize she must have just taken a shot of insulin. Her doctor warned me of the dangerous mood swings that can occur with an overdose of insulin. I have noticed more frequent swings into anger and irritability, but this is by far the worst outburst I've yet seen.

"Moman, no!" I say, but these are the wrong words. She sees it as a challenge to her authority.

"Savannah, this death is on you. It could have been avoided if only you'd obeyed."

I frown as she lowers the syringe to Dion's arm. It's empty. What is she planning to do? Then it hits me. She's going to inject an air bubble into him and try to cause an embolism that could stop his heart from working correctly. It's a crazy measure, something we had just seen in a movie on our last "family time" night, and I'm not at all sure it will work. But the mere fact she even thinks of it is deeply disturbing.

"What are you doing, Moman? Think, please."

I reach for my mother's hand to stop her, jostling the syringe so it falls to the floor. Moman turns and strikes me again, knocking me back into a low coffee table. I stumble against it and fall to the floor.

"Albert, put him to sleep!" Moman cries.

By the time I regain my feet, Albert has Dion in a sleeper hold and is slowly choking the life out of him. Even when Dion stops struggling, Albert doesn't let go. Instead, he drags the man out of the parlor.

Moman turns to me. "Upstairs, to your room, now. We will never speak of this, and you will never disobey me again."

I turn and flee the parlor, but instead of going to my room, I run out the door with only one look back.

T RIP'S whole body was tight with tension. Savannah's story had a lurid quality to it that told him it was more than some made-up fairytale meant to throw them off. It was too detailed, the fear on her face too real, to let him think it was anything other than true.

No one in the room spoke for a long moment while Savannah stared into her coffee mug. Finally, Mitzi stirred.

"How is it that the FBI is looking for you? Do they think you killed Dion?"

"I don't know. I doubt it. With my mother on the campaign trail, it'll soon be noticed I'm not at her side. Before I left the state, back when I still dared to get online, I saw a news story in which she spun a tale of having sent me off on holiday to Europe. With the election a little more than a month away, people will begin to wonder why I haven't returned. I suspect she'll have recruited her pet FBI agent to track me down and bring me back into the fold, and I shudder to think what she'll threaten me with to make me stay. And after the election—"

"How do you know she has a pet FBI agent?" Mitzi asked.

"Because when I ran, I went to the FBI. Dion and I had done an online search and found out the FBI is responsible for investigating corrupt politicians. Even in my shock and horror, I knew I could not trust the New

Orleans police, so I went straight to the FBI's field office. I walked in and told the whole story to Agent Emmanuel Laurencett. He listened to every word, then told me he would take me to a safe house where I could await the depositions, hearings, and trial that would surely soon be in the works. Then he put me in his car and drove me right back to *Moman's* house.

"Once I realized where we were going, I confronted him. When he confirmed it, I went a little crazy. I jumped out of his car at a stoplight and ran again. I ran to some activist friends of Dion's I had met once, and they helped me hide in the city. The plan was to go to the press, but Laurencett was there at every turn. I don't know what he told them, but every time I tried to get an interview with someone I was turned away at reception, or it was apparent they were waiting for security and I had to run. Once, I walked into a bank to withdraw cash, and he pulled up outside moments after I'd walked away. If I hadn't been disguised to look like a Yankee tourist, I would have been caught.

"We realized I had to leave the city, and Dion's friends helped me. They drove me all the way to Shreveport to make sure I got away. When I called to check in about a week later, Laurencett answered their phone. I don't know if they're alive or dead. I hung up before he could issue any threats. It was the only thing I could think to do. If I didn't listen to any demands, surely he wouldn't follow through with a threat I never even heard. I've been running ever since."

"Oh, sweetheart," Momma said, reaching across the table to capture her hand.

Mitzi frowned. "Let me get this straight. You've been running on a few assumptions, the first being Dion is dead.

The second being your mother will somehow hurt you if you come back?'"

"I do know Dion is dead," Savannah said, her tone defensive. "There was a moment right before I ran out the door when I looked back and saw Albert. He'd lain Dion out on the foyer floor and was checking his pulse. He looked up at me, and the look on his face told me everything. I've known Albert all my life. I know he would kill if he thought he was protecting *Moman*.

"As for what would happen if I came back? I don't know. What I do know is I couldn't look at her knowing she caused Dion's death, and she will not allow anything to get between her and her goal of becoming governor. The best-case scenario is life in a virtual prison, my every move controlled by her. The worst case, a fatal accident in my near future. I don't see any middle ground, and I'm not inclined to test either theory. I'd hoped to escape into Canada, or somehow fake my death, but I've really just been winging it, hoping something will give. Being here this past week…. I had actually hoped this place could be the hole Savannah Montault de Saint-Cirié disappeared into, never to be heard from again." She looked at all the faces around the table, her gaze coming to rest on Trip's. "I like it here."

Trip did not break eye contact with her, letting his gaze lock onto her hazel-green eyes. He still didn't know what to say, but he did know he wanted her to stay. He shuddered to think about the trauma she'd endured just to cover the distance between her life in New Orleans and her life here.

Mitzi leaned forward in her chair, drawing everyone's attention. "I have to tell Sheriff Jonas about this. I have no choice."

"What? No!" Savannah pushed back from the table in terror. "I tell you my story because you say I can trust you, but I know I will die if the law becomes involved. I know it."

"Sheriff Jonas is a good man, old school. He can't abide corruption. That's one of the reasons he was willing to hire me."

Trip watched the shadow of pain cross Mitzi's face, as it always did when the topic of her history came up.

"I was once hunted down for a crime I didn't commit and in clearing my name I took down a quarter of Denver's police force, corruption that spread all the way to the Chief of Police. Even though I was in the right, it became impossible for me to stay in Denver and work with men who were afraid I would betray them. Sheriff Jonas hired me because he admired my loyalty to the law, to justice. He will listen to your story, and he'll know what to do."

Daddy nodded his agreement. "Casper Jonas is one of the best men I know. He won't do anything to hurt you. He'll help keep you safe."

"We all will," Trip said. He didn't trust himself to say any more, though. Not until he had a moment's privacy with Savannah Dawn. He didn't think now was the time to declare just how invested he was in keeping her safe.

"Savannah," Momma said, and something about her tone brought everyone's attention to her. "When I first met you, I knew something terrible had happened to you and was still going on in your life. I didn't know what, but I felt compelled to invite you into our lives because I *knew* this was where you were meant to be. Stay with us now. Don't go. We can help you, if you'll let us."

chapter
seventeen

S avannah looked down at Maddy's words. It was as if the woman knew what she had only decided moments ago.

She had to leave. It wasn't safe for this family, these people she had come to consider friends. There was no way she could bring the hell of her life down on them. They might do their best to protect her, but in her heart, she knew there was no way they could stop a man like Laurencett, who had all the power of the FBI behind him.

They would all pay too high a price if she allowed them to talk her into staying, and she couldn't bear the thought of bringing pain and worse to these wonderful people.

She nodded without looking up.

"Stay," Maddy repeated. "Please."

To cover the tremor in her hands, Savannah raised her mug to her lips and drained the last of the coffee. "Well," she said. "Thank you all for listening to my tale of woe, and for your kind offers of help. You have no idea how much it means to me. Now, if I am going to stay, I had better get over to the chow hall and see what kind of chaos the men have left for me. Please excuse me."

She pushed her chair farther away from the table and stood, bringing both men to their feet. Unable to meet anyone's gaze, she turned and strode from the room as if she were on a mission. And she was—just not the one she claimed to be on.

Out the door and across the yard before anyone could say a word, she didn't slow until she was on the porch of her cabin. *The cook's cabin*, she corrected. It wasn't hers. It wasn't home. Once inside the door, she took a breath and steadied herself.

What now? If she out and out ran, she'd probably have Mitzi on her trail before she could get out the driveway. She'd have to play it cool, make an excuse to go to town, then just keep going. In the meantime, she could pack her few belongings and leave the kitchen in order.

As she walked to the closet and opened it, she felt more than a twinge of guilt at the thought of leaving Maddy in the lurch again, but it couldn't be helped.

Savannah hauled her bag out from the bottom of the closet and set it on the bed, propping it open before turning back to slide a few of her blouses off their hangers.

"What are you doing?"

She froze at the sound of Trip's voice behind her and hugged the clothing to her chest before she turned around.

He stood in the doorway, the firm set of his jaw giving away his determination, but she didn't think he was angry with her.

"Preparation," she said, attempting a light shrug of her shoulders that came off in a kind of spastic jerk. "Just in case I gotta leave in a hurry. You understand, *wi?*"

"I understand you're fixin' to run," he said, crossing the room to stand before her, invading her personal space.

"Can't say as I blame you. But I hope. . . we all hope you'll stay. Give us a chance to protect you."

A shiver raced up her spine as Trip reached out and tipped her chin up so she was forced to look him in the eye.

"No one can protect me," she whispered. "Not until I leave the country, and even then I'm in danger, I think. I . . . . Don't ask me to stay, Trip. I already want so much to call this place *mô koté*, my home, but I fear for you as much as for me. It's too dangerous."

"Don't you worry about us, Miss Dawn. The Thomas family knows how to take care of ourselves and those we care about. I promise you, we're not just dumb country hicks. And Mitzi was a police detective in Denver. She knows stuff about big cities and corruption. Between her and Sheriff Jonas, they'll know what to do."

Savannah's heart sank to her toes as she listened to Trip's impassioned plea. He was so sure of himself. She didn't know how he would be able to follow through on his promise, yet the look in his eye was so sincere, she couldn't bring herself to argue anymore.

"You're sweet, Trip." She reached up to grasp his hand and pressed a kiss into his palm. "Perhaps you are right."

"I know I am," he said, before gently releasing her clothes from her grip and setting them on the bed so he could wrap her in a tight hug. She laid her cheek against his chest and heard his strong heartbeat, the sound its own kind of comfort. She let her arms slide around his waist and—for the moment, anyway—let herself believe he was right.

Just as the embrace started to get awkward, Trip released her, setting her back from him so he could look her in the eye.

"Momma said I should help you in the kitchen."

"*Me non*," she said. "Surely there's not much to do."

The look he gave her suggested she was underestimating the ranch hands' ability to leave havoc in their wake. "Come, let's see."

To her dismay, the kitchen looked a bit like a tornado had blown through. There was a puddle of coffee under the coffee pot, and it had tracked down the front of the cabinet as though someone had forgotten to put the carafe under the drip.

Empty bagel wrappers suggested she hadn't prepped enough to sate their appetites, and there were dirty knives in the sink, along with wadded-up paper towels and crumbs on the counter, and one tub of cream cheese left sitting on the island countertop.

All in all, it wasn't as bad as it could have been, but it was a bit disappointing to see Jax hadn't taken the time to clean a bit better.

Trip stepped ahead of her and pushed open the door to the chow hall. His sharp intake of breath told her that room was in much worse shape.

She followed, prepared to determine what needed to be done before she could in all conscience depart the ranch.

Trip surveyed the chow hall, his hands on his hips, proud of his part in cleaning it up. He would never call himself domestic, but his daddy had drilled into him how to clean. It was not a skill his mother had worried overly much about, but Daddy's days in the Army left him a fastidious man.

A giggle from behind him threatened to pop his bubble. "What?" he said. "It's clean."

"*Wi.*"

Savannah's smile was contagious, and he grinned back even as he gestured to the room. "I told you I could clean."

"Oh, *wi*. I didn't doubt. It's only the way men expect a pat on the head for their effort after cleaning one room. They don't think how women do this work every day with no reward except their own pleasure in a job well done."

Trip wanted to be offended but couldn't do it in the face of her smile. "Well," he protested at last, "it's not like I expect kudos for fixing a hole in a fence or bucking a load of hay . . . ."

She held up a hand to forestall his argument. "I shouldn't judge. It's only—" She broke off whatever she was going to say, but he wasn't going to let her off the hook that easily.

"Ah now. You started, you gotta tell me."

Biting her lips together, she shook her head. Before he could think too hard about it, he reached out and grabbed her by the waist, intent on tickling the truth out of her.

She laughed and pulled away from him, edging toward the kitchen. "You are *adorabl*," she said, before backing through the swinging door.

Trip chased her, the desire to hold her the only thing on his mind. He nearly struck her with the door when he pushed through, surprised to find her facing him, the light of mischief fading from her eyes as their gazes locked.

Without hesitation, he closed the distance between them and put his hands on her hips again, this time with a firm grip intended to hold her still. She leaned into him on tiptoe, brushing her lips against his. Her fingers curled against the short hairs at the nape of his neck and he deepened the kiss, tasting coffee on her tongue.

Settling her even closer, he moved his hands to the

small of her back to enjoy the sensation of her pliant body fitted like a puzzle piece against his.

When she broke the kiss, it was a long moment before he opened his eyes to see her gazing up at him, her eyes shining with some emotion he couldn't name. It wasn't upset or accusation—he knew he hadn't read her wrong—but there was definitely something going on.

"What is it?" he asked, then pressed a kiss against the top of her head. "Tell me what's wrong."

"Nothing," she whispered, but he was pretty sure those were unshed tears in her eyes.

Before he could press her, the sound of the door to the chow hall opening reached them, and she jumped back, putting a respectable distance between them.

"Trip! You in here, boy?"

"Yessir," he said, without breaking eye contact with Savannah. "We're just finishing up."

"Good. Then you can tell me what the devil this certified letter from the insurance company is all about."

That made him look toward the door as Daddy pushed through, waving a sheaf of documents. "What?"

Just like that, the moment was gone. He hardly had a chance to glance at Savannah before Daddy herded him out the side door and across the yard to the house.

chapter
eighteen

The remainder of the week was a kind of torture for Savannah as she tried at every turn to come up with an excuse to go to town. Every time she was foiled, sometimes blatantly, by Maddy.

When she said she needed fresh greens from the farm, Maddy suggested Trip drive her. When she tried to load her bag into her car, Maddy was in the yard, hanging out laundry or cleaning up the flower beds in preparation for fall. The woman seemed to have a sixth sense that knew when she was readying herself to make a run for it.

It terrified her that Sheriff Jonas hadn't been out to see her yet, that he was doing online research that would alert Laurencett to her whereabouts. Or perhaps he had contacted the FBI directly and it was only a matter of time before they rolled up in their black SUVs and carted her away.

Left to its own devices, her fear led her imagination on a wild ride.

The only good thing about her failure to depart manifested in the form of a handsome cowboy who'd been smiling a lot more since their kiss in the kitchen. That moment burned in her memory as the single-most bitter-sweet pleasure in her recent history, but it was just as well they'd been unable to recapture it.

She'd intended for it to be a goodbye kiss—she'd fully expected to be on the road mere hours later—but in her memory it tasted like forever.

Wishful thinking. A daydream to counter her rising fear. But what a daydream. She could tell he shared her pleasure in the memory, the way he caught her gaze from across the yard. More than once he started over to speak to her, only to have someone or some situation interrupt. Which was all to the better, really. If they didn't get a chance to make that kind of connection again, it would be that much easier to leave when she found her chance.

It would be hard enough to go as it was.

But she had a plan by Sunday morning. Maddy always left early for church, and this Sunday was no exception.

After watching her leave, Savannah waited an agonizing fifteen minutes before grabbing her bag off the bed and hurrying to her Chevy Citation. Every noise she made rang out in the still morning air. The way the driver's door creaked on its hinges then had to be slammed to close properly. The cranking of the tired engine that hadn't been run since her arrival. For a moment she was afraid it wouldn't start at all. She exhaled heavily when it finally caught, accompanied by a cloud of white smoke.

So much for a stealthy departure. It would have been better to wait until everyone had left the ranch.

Easing the car into first gear, she let out the clutch in time to see Trip hurrying down the stairs, untucked shirt-tails flying as he ran toward her. She waved, fully intending to just drive on by, but he skidded to a stop in front of the car, forcing her to jam on the brakes or hit him.

"Hold up!" he said, putting his hands on the hood of the car as if to push her back into her parking space.

"I'm just running to the store," she called out through the windshield.

"I'm coming with you." He met and held her gaze with determination.

She exhaled. There was no hope of dissuading him. If she bolted when he came around the passenger side of the car, he'd just follow her in one of the ranch vehicles. When he climbed in, folding his frame awkwardly to fit into the cramped space, she pretended he was a welcome addition to her shopping party.

"I needed an ingredient for the dish I'm bringing this afternoon," she said while he tucked in his shirt, the activity clumsy in the limited space. She studiously avoided watching him. In another circumstance, the thought of the loose buttons of his 501s would be too tempting even without actually seeing his hands touch places she wanted to touch herself.

"Uh huh," he said, finally buckling in. He motioned up the driveway.

Without a further word, she released the clutch and sent the Citation lurching up the hill. "Sorry," she said after the bumpy start. "I only recently learned to drive a stick."

"You're doing fine," he said, the voice of encouragement.

She didn't want to lie anymore, so she remained silent as they climbed the hill and made their way to town. The only words that passed between them involved what direction to turn once they hit the highway and again when she questioned whether the tiny market across from the truck stop was the only place in town to get groceries. They pulled up in Main Street Market's lot having exchanged less than ten words each.

She hesitated. She didn't have any ingredients in mind, and Trip would know she'd been planning to run for it. *Bondjé*, he probably already knew. He'd beaten her at poker —he obviously knew how to read her tells.

That didn't stop her from trying to figure out how to ditch him at the store. It wouldn't take much, would it? Send him to the far aisle for some random item while she slipped back out the side door?

"So, what's the secret ingredient?" he asked, waving a hand at the store as they crossed the small parking lot. "Is it even something we'll have in town?"

"I. . . ah, used all the curry powder, and . . . ." She took in the signs describing the sections of the store as they walked inside, trying to find the two that were farthest apart. "I need some. . . cream cheese. Can you find it for me?"

Trip gave her a knowing look, hesitating two beats before moving in the direction she indicated. She headed across the front of the store, making for the tiny spice section, discreetly watching for him to turn down the aisle.

The moment he cleared her line of vision, she hurried toward the door, only to barrel straight into the man coming through.

TRIP STOOD STARING at the miniscule dairy section, trying to locate the right kind of cream cheese. He hadn't known there would be so many choices—not when the entire section only held about a dozen types of dairy products. Did she want it in a tub or a box? Whipped or block?

Regular or Neufchâtel? Whatever the heck that meant. He grabbed a block and a tub, then headed back up front to ask her to be more specific.

"What the heck is New-fat-chel cream cheese?" he asked as he rounded the end cap. . . only to see no one. A quick glance out the window proved Savannah's ugly Chevy was still in the lot, so he headed toward the far side of the store, checking each aisle as he passed. It appeared the only other person in the store was the clerk, who idly flipped through his phone without paying any attention to his surroundings.

The sound of brakes squealing out on the highway reached him. When he looked outside, he saw a driver hanging out the window of his car, making an exasperated gesture at a man and woman crossing in front of him. It was Savannah with some man who looked like a truck driver pulling her after him as he headed for the truck stop.

Cursing, Trip dropped the cream cheese and ran for the door, his eyes fixed on Savannah. He never saw what hit him on the back of the head and knocked him flat to the pavement.

"Scream and my partner will kill whoever looks our way," the truck driver told her, and Savannah had no reason not to believe him. Still, it was hard to keep up as he dragged her across the highway and up to the truck idling at the fuel island.

She didn't know anything about big rigs, but she recognized the Volvo emblem on the grille, and it was easy to see the flatbed trailer was empty of cargo.

The fat, greasy-haired white man pushed her up the

metal steps into the cab on the driver's side of the truck. She tried to quickly climb over the shifter and exit the passenger door, but he had a hold on her ankle before she even cleared the driver's seat. She ended up on her butt on the floor between the seats among candy wrappers and empty paper coffee cups.

By the time she regained her feet the truck was in motion, the driver shifting through gears. He paused at the driveway leading out onto the highway, and she lunged for the door again. It opened under her hand and she fell forward, coming face to face with a black man who had a broken-toothed grin for her. As he climbed into the truck, she backpedaled, ramming the gear shift into her thigh before bouncing off the driver's seat.

The new arrival pushed her back into the sleeper of the truck, overpowering her efforts to fight her way forward. The last glimpse she had of the town of Syracuse was the parking lot of the store she'd just left behind and a small crowd of people standing around Trip as he staggered to his feet, one hand on the back of his head, looking around. She could read the desperation of his actions, and thought she heard him calling her name over the sound of the diesel engine accelerating as they pulled out of the truck stop.

She didn't bother asking who these men were. It didn't matter. The only thing that mattered was where they were taking her—and she didn't think that was to church.

The man shoved her and she lost her balance when the backs of her knees hit what turned out to be a mattress. She scrambled away from him until she felt a cushioned wall at her shoulders. When he drew a curtain across the space between the seats the light vanished so completely, blind panic froze her in place until her eyes began to adjust to the gloom.

"What do you want?" she asked when she realized he was still standing near the curtain, braced against the motion of the truck. She thought he was looking at her, but she couldn't be sure.

"Plenty of things I can't have. One of them being a good, close look at your nekkid body with those dangerous curves. But the man with the money said you ought not be harmed, so all I get to do is watch you. Unless of course," he paused meaningfully, "you decide you're bored. We got a long trip ahead of us, and I don't see near enough of my wife."

She shuddered and pushed herself farther into the corner.

"The man with the money, I assume you mean Laurencett?"

The man didn't respond, but finally moved to sit near her on the ratty mattress.

"Shame you're off the menu," he said, lifting a hand as though to touch her hair.

She snapped her teeth at him and he pulled away. "You know he'll kill you if you touch me," she said, trying to put her best snarl into her voice. She knew no such thing. She was banking on her mother not wanting to risk her arrival back in New Orleans looking like she'd. . . well, been kidnapped and raped by a couple dirty truck drivers. "At the very least, you'll not see your money."

Whichever threat it was, one of them worked. Before she knew what he was up to, he'd produced a set of hand-cuffs—the fuzzy kind no doubt found in a sex toy store—and slapped one side around her ankle, then put the other around his.

"I gotta drive tonight, darlin', so I need my sleep. This here is only to warn me if you get up to no good, you hear? I'm a light sleeper. You move, I'll know it." He proceeded to fluff a pillow and curl up on the other side of the mattress. If not for the feeling of being watched in the dim light glowing around the curtain and the edges of some kind of fabric that blacked out the windows, she'd have believed he'd dropped off into sleep.

It surprised her when, not long after, she heard a soft snore from that side of the sleeper. Not quite able to believe someone could fall asleep so swiftly, she still gave in to her curiosity sooner than was prudent and carefully pulled at the edge of the vinyl fabric around the window, trying to see out. A snap closure gave way, then another, allowing her to lift a corner. She peered out to see the Kansas prairie rolling by.

She thought they were heading west, though she couldn't be sure, and wondered what the plan was.

Then she cursed herself for all kinds of a fool. Why had she decided to run from the ranch? Even if Laurencett had acted on some clue given away by Mitzi's search, the odds of any of his minions finding their way out to the ranch were slim to none. Very few people in town knew she was out there, and those who did knew her by a different name—one Laurencett had no reason to expect her to use.

Instead, she had run straight into the arms of his men.

To top it off, Trip had been hurt trying to follow her. She knew she was lucky the man hadn't killed him, but knowing he was in pain because of her was a bone in the throat, impossible to swallow.

After a while, she let the fabric fall back into place and simply stared into the gloom, listening to all the creaks and rattles and the rumble of the diesel engine.

chapter
nineteen

"What do you mean you won't be able to trace her?" Trip asked. He threw down the package of frozen corn he'd been holding to the back of his head and stood up to pace the nearly empty diner. "She can't have just disappeared without a trace."

Mitzi's voice filtered over the speaker of his phone, echoing into the room. "You said yourself you saw a guy pulling her toward the truck stop. If he put her in a vehicle, no one has come forward who saw him do it. It'll take time to see if the security cameras caught anything. You said she doesn't have a phone, so we have nothing to trace. Unless we can find someone who got a good look at the man or the make and model of a vehicle, we can only guess what happened. I think we have to go on the assumption she's being taken back to her mother in New Orleans."

"What about the FBI agent? Can't you reach out to one of your friends?"

"I already did," Mitzi said. His sister-in-law had two contacts in the Bureau. "Agent Maxon said he hadn't heard anything about this Laurencett, but he'd do some discreet digging. Agent Sanderson said she'd served a little time in the New Orleans office leading up to her stint in Houston. She'd gotten the feeling Laurencett was a little slimy, but not enough she'd wanted to look closer. She had other fish to fry at the time. But she said she'd see what she could find out. If there's any chatter about him regarding the mayor's daughter, one of them will turn it up. In the meantime, I'm getting together what information I can and starting the paperwork to initiate a missing-presumed-abducted BOLO. If I can tie it to her being a person of interest in a crime, it should net more eyes on the road, and with luck we'll find her before they take her too far."

"And then?" Trip had to ask.

Mitzi sighed. "It's far too early to tell. If we get her back, we'll still have to deal with keeping her away from her mother—and from corrupt elements of the agency that's supposed to keep her safe. There's no telling what will happen at this point."

"But you're not going to give up on finding her, are you?"

"No, Trip, I'm not. She's in a rough situation, and I certainly can't see leaving her to it just because finding her will be hard."

"Thanks," Trip said. "I was hoping you'd say that."

Mitzi didn't say anything for a meaningful moment. Then, "If you were my husband, I'd be worried you were planning to take matters into your own hands. I trust you'll be smarter than your brother and let the professionals handle this."

It hadn't exactly occurred to him that he might be able to do something about this himself until she'd warned him against it.

"Just what do you think I could do from here?" he asked.

"Nice try, Trip. I'm not going to give you any ideas. Just stay put and I'll keep you posted, all right?"

He didn't answer. His mind was already racing.

"Trip?"

"Yeah, no. Thanks for everything, Mitzi. I owe you."

"Trip—"

"I'll talk to you later," he said, cutting off the warning she was ramping up to give him.

Five seconds later he was driving Savannah's Citation back to the ranch. Thirty minutes after that he was up in his room, opening a duffle bag and tossing in a handful of clothes.

Daddy met him at the bottom of the stairs when he came back down.

"What are you up to, son?"

Feeling a bit like a teenager caught sneaking out, he shifted from foot to foot, avoiding his father's gaze. "Nothing," he said, and made to step around him to get to the door.

"Mitzi called, told me what happened. Said she was worried you were fixin' to do something stupid."

"Define stupid," Trip said, then threw out a hand in exasperation. "Some guy just grabbed her, Daddy. I don't know where they are, what direction they headed, but I don't have to see the clouds to know when it's raining on my head. They're taking her to New Orleans, and she's going to need my help. I can't help her from Kansas."

"What do you think you'll be able to do that Mitzi and the proper authorities can't?"

"You're going to ask me that, Daddy? After you ran off to New Mexico to save Kylie when you didn't even know where she'd last been sighted? You weren't going to leave her safety up to the authorities. Why should I trust them with Savannah's life?"

"What is she to you? To us?" Daddy's voice was a mixture of hard and curious, leaving room for Trip to hope he could play up to his old man's sense of honor.

"Besides a friend? Besides giving Momma a break by making some of the best food I've ever eaten? Besides being the first woman who makes me forget about Kate? Who makes me laugh, and—" he stopped and cleared his throat. "Besides all that, we owe it to her to help."

Daddy's brows raised in surprise. "How do you figure?"

"She stayed here to help us as much as to help herself. Sure, we gave her a place to hide, but our family is the reason she was found. If Momma hadn't convinced her to stay, she'd have been back on the road hours after she arrived. If Mitzi hadn't searched for her, given away her location, she'd still be free. Maybe these guys would have caught up with her eventually, but they got to her now because we failed her—because *I* failed her."

Something flickered behind his father's implacable expression. Trip pressed on, knowing he'd made a connection. "So, I'm going to New Orleans to try to save her. I don't know how, or even where to look, but I'll figure something out on the way."

"*We'll* figure something out," Daddy said, and Trip did a double-take.

"I'm sorry, what?"

"You heard me. Give me five minutes and I'll have a bag ready."

TRIP AWAKENED when Daddy's truck slowed. He opened his eyes and rubbed them as he looked around to see where they were. Traffic had been light, being a Sunday and all, and they'd made minimal stops thanks to the extra fuel tank in the back of Daddy's big Dodge Ram 3500. The biggest delays they'd run into were the infernal road construction sites that gave Trip the impression half the country was in the middle of road repairs, which was probably just as well, because the rest of the country appeared to have been struck by some kind of asphalt eating troll that left chewed up highway in its wake, making true sleep impossible.

Trip had driven the stretch between Jolly, Texas and Shreveport, Louisiana, waking Daddy from his combat nap only for the nightmare of navigating through Dallas and Fort Worth, where even the GPS had trouble thanks to all the construction. Then he'd fallen into an uneasy sleep, plagued by the rough passage and thoughts of what Savannah was enduring while they raced to her rescue.

This slowdown was different from the other brief delays, though. Daddy pulled off the interstate and into a giant truck stop. Rather than pulling up to the fuel island, he drove around the back. Trip checked the time on his phone and saw it was 2:00AM, local time. He refreshed the weather app to learn the current temperature in La Place, Louisiana was seventy-five degrees.

They were almost to New Orleans.

Passing rows of semis, Trip watched Daddy's gaze sweep the lot as though his head was on a swivel. He was looking for something, someone in particular. Finally, in the corner farthest from the lights of the building, a man stepped out from between two trucks and waved them down.

Judging by the ball cap, blue button-down, short-sleeved shirt, and worn blue jeans, he looked like just another truck driver, but something in his bearing said he was. . . more. A military man, like Daddy. And though the clothes were nondescript, they were clean and fit so well they might have been tailor-made.

At the man's direction, Daddy pulled in front of a red Kenworth semi-tractor and shut off his pickup. He climbed out and Trip scrambled to join him, joints protesting his long inactivity.

All around them, truck engines roared as they idled to provide air conditioning for their sleeping drivers, and Trip realized it was an ideal place to have a private meeting. The noise was enough to prevent anyone from overhearing a conversation—even with top-notch spy equipment like in the movies. It made him wonder why they needed to have a clandestine meeting, and with whom.

He vaguely remembered Daddy talking on the phone while he'd tried to sleep. In and amongst calls that were certainly demands from Momma and maybe even Mitzi to know what was going on, he now remembered there was also something about "filling a dance card," "debts to be repaid," and a "special package." In his semi-dream-state consciousness, he hadn't thought to eavesdrop. Now he wished he had.

There were no introductions. The man just ducked back between the noisy trucks and Daddy followed, giving no indication whether Trip should come with them or not. After a moment's hesitation, his curiosity got the better of him and he fell in line, hot on their heels. When they rounded the back of the trailer, he saw a garment bag— one of those fancy zip-up kinds like a tuxedo would be stored in—folded atop a large duffle bag on the ground. Still without speaking, the man handed it to Trip, then took a knee beside the duffle and opened it. Daddy peered inside, moved a few items around, then nodded to the man, who closed the bag and stood. They shook hands, then the other man sketched a salute.

"See you tonight," he said, then turned and vanished into the darkness.

Daddy hefted the bag, then lifted his chin, indicating Trip should head back to the pickup.

Once they were back in the cab, the duffle bag on the seat between them, Trip opened his mouth to ask one of the hundreds of questions racing through his mind.

"What was that all about?" was the first one to come out of his mouth.

"Jimmy owed me a favor. Open the bag, son. There's a manilla envelope inside with intel we need."

While Daddy headed back out to the parking lot by the truck stop store, Trip opened the bag. As they passed under a light pole, a glint of metal revealed a pair of pistols in holsters sitting atop several boxes of ammunition. He blinked in surprise. These were not Daddy's trusty Ruger Vaquero single-action Colt-style .45 revolvers or even his Colt M1911. These looked like brand new .45 caliber semi-automatics, and there was enough ammo to make headlines if Daddy hit his targets—and Colton Thomas Jr. always hit his targets.

"Good lord, Daddy," Trip muttered.

"Just being prepared, son. The envelope?"

"I don't know who you think you're going to shoot at, given the odds anyone likely to shoot back will be law enforcement. FBI and the like. Not to mention, I don't understand why you didn't just bring your own pistols."

"I did bring mine. These are for you, son."

Daddy gave him a moment to let that sink in—and Trip needed it. He knew about firearms, had been around them all his life. He'd shot every weapon on the ranch enough to be proficient, and some of his best bonding moments with his father had come from shooting coyotes and old tin cans up on the prairie. Usually they shot a 30-

30, or Daddy's Winchester, but since the summer's excitement of Tim's past coming back to haunt him and Kylie and Jax's kidnapping, they'd put a bit more focus on the handguns. Still, Trip had never seriously considered he might have to shoot a human. The thought chilled him more than the frigid air blowing from the pickup's AC.

"The envelope?" Daddy said again. Trip reluctantly tore his gaze away from the weapons to focus on the manilla envelope. His fingers stiff with tension, he pulled it out and opened it. "What does it say?"

"It says there's a party tonight."

chapter
twenty

Trip stepped out of the smallish shower and wrapped a towel around his waist, then used a white washcloth to wipe the condensation from the mirror. Like the bureau squeezed in at the foot of the two double beds in the room beyond, it was a close fit between the tub surround, toilet and vanity. It wasn't that the room was dingy or even cheaply furnished, it was just cramped, especially for folks the size of him and his daddy.

In fact, the quaint motel on Ursulines Avenue they'd checked into in the wee hours of the morning lacked any of the voodoo charm he'd expected to find in New Orleans. . . if he'd ever stopped to think about cheap places to stay in New Orleans. The realization he was really here hit him full force as he gazed at his own reflection, noting the look in his eyes that struck even him as a little wild.

They had grabbed a few hours of rack time serenaded by a crotchety air conditioning unit, and Trip had awoken to the sound of his father taking a shower. It was 4:00PM according to the bedside clock, and when Daddy had emerged, he'd gestured for Trip to clean up next.

"Take your time, son," had been his only comment.

He stared at his face in the mirror, still pink from the shave and scrubbing under hot water he'd given it, and wondered if he was up to the task of what lay ahead.

The intel in the envelope had outlined a plan that was either genius or the most bone-headed thing he'd ever heard. He was a cowboy for Pete's sake, not an actor who could pull off the role required of him.

He opened the door, ready to argue once more for a different plan, but hesitated. His father was dressed to the nines in an all-white, three-piece linen suit, the only splash of color being the black bowtie and matching kerchief in the breast pocket. His graying hair, usually covered by his Stetson, was combed back from his forehead and plastered into place with some kind of gel or pomade. He looked distinguished and ready to take care of business.

Trip's gaze flickered to the garment bag hanging on the hook that passed for a closet in the room. A matching suit waited for him.

"Get dressed, son. We're supposed to meet Jimmy at the Roosevelt. The car he's sending for us will be here in half an hour." With that, Colton pulled his phone out of his pocket and stepped out of the room and into the narrow hallway.

Trip began to dress, feeling a bit like a teenager getting ready for his first prom. Except he'd never gone to prom. He and Kate had fought about it—she'd wanted to go and he hadn't—and she'd gone with Bradley Corman. Even his Sunday best wasn't as fancy as this get-up. He felt like a fraud. He was out of his element and possibly in way over his head. The only thing he could hold onto was that coming here had been his idea. And if he'd been on his own, well. . . he'd probably still be on his way—without a plan.

He finished buttoning the dress shirt, marveling more than a little at the light feel and loose cut he didn't think would cling to him in the heat and humidity. The only suits he'd ever worn were heavy wool and scratchy, surely heat-stroke inducing in southern climates, but this felt like it would be more comfortable even than his Wranglers and a t-shirt.

On top of that, he was starting to feel like he might possibly pull off the part he was being asked to play. At least in the costume department.

He was studying the black bowtie, wondering how to tie it, when Daddy walked back in the room.

He eyed his father in the mirror, deciding to try once again to argue the plan. "Daddy, I don't know if I can pull this off. Don't you think it's a little insane?" His father didn't respond, so he kept at it. "Why can't we just say we are who we really are? You're an old army buddy of Jimmy's, and I'm your son. Why this charade?"

Daddy shook his head as he walked over, turned Trip to face him, and took the tie away. He carefully flipped it over Trip's head so it draped down his front, then proceeded to tie the silken scrap into a perfect bow.

"We have to assume Savannah has been questioned about her whereabouts, who she was associating with and why," he said as he worked. "Doubt, but don't know if she would deliberately put us in harm's way. From what I hear about her mother, we'd be smarter to play it safe. Without a cover story in place, might as well advertise we're a rescue party."

"But a security detail? What do I know about protecting people?"

Colton gave one final tweak to the tie then lifted his eyes to meet his son's gaze. "If you care anything at all about Savannah, you'll make this count. We have to get on the inside to find her, and this is the only way on such short notice. Focus on the plan and you'll do fine."

Trip was struck by the way this moment was going down. It was like a twisted parody of the father giving his son a pep talk on the eve of his first serious date—what could have been a touching snapshot of bonding between the two men. And in a sense, it was bonding of a totally different sort.

"I do care about her, Daddy. A lot. I'm not sure I'd be here otherwise. I'd probably have left it to Mitzi's contacts at the FBI to take care of things. Part of me still wonders if that's not the smarter course of action."

His father's gaze intensified, and Trip was reminded of that time he'd ridden his horse all the way into town just to buy some candy with his allowance. He'd only been five at the time and had gotten lost on the way back to the ranch. His father had chewed him out royally once he'd been found, near dark, wandering in the Petersen's fallow field, his horse gorging on the clover cover crop. Relentless lessons on orienteering followed to make sure Trip could always find his way home. It wasn't until Trip turned thirty that Daddy confessed he'd been frightened out of his mind with worry.

Now Trip thought he knew what that look meant. Daddy was worried too, but there was going to be a lesson in all this, and Trip thought he knew it would be about having confidence in himself.

"We're here now, son. No harm in measuring the lay of the land. Don't have to do more than that if there's any chance of the night getting out of hand." He put both hands on Trip's shoulders. "I like Miss Savannah too. She's got moxie to have come as far as she did, and I hate to think of the part our family played in getting her caught. She's smart, but I'm not sure she'll be able to hide her heart from her mother's political backers for too long—and that's where she'll face the most danger. If her mother thinks Savannah will betray her, I wouldn't put it past the woman to silence her forever."

Trip thought about the night he and Savannah played cards, and he agreed she didn't have much of a poker face. He also recalled the concern—the fear he'd felt for her safety that had driven him to head down here in the first place. "You're right, of course. If we just see how she's being treated, what's the worst that can happen?"

Daddy gave his shoulders a brief squeeze, and Trip understood what his father didn't say: there were half a hundred things that could go wrong.

"It's a risk," he said, confirming Trip's suspicions. "For everyone concerned."

Trip ran his hands through his hair, then self-consciously smoothed it back in place. "I can't say I understand why Jimmy is willing to take this risk."

Daddy looked away, then stepped aside to peer out the window.

"I don't like to talk about the things I did in the war. Try not to even think about it. Momma helps with that. But Jimmy. . . saving him was the biggest of mixed blessings."

He sighed heavily, and Trip thought that was all he was going to say. He was thoroughly surprised when he continued.

"My team was scouting this village we suspected was an enemy base when the rest of the squad got pinned down in a ravine. We could hear the gunfire, but the radio was hit, so we didn't have. . . we didn't know." Daddy cleared his throat and resumed in an attempt at a brisk tone. "The squad had walked smack into a trap, a dozen well-armed VC surrounding their position, with three enemy sniper nests just picking them off one at a time. Jimmy, as sergeant and head of the squad, tried to hold them off, but it was grim.

"By dumb luck, my spotter Corky and I had the high ground when we topped the ridge, and I had a perfect view of their snipers' nests—all three of them. Wildly improbable shots, and by a miracle, I made them. Also managed to hit their leader and in the chaos, the squad cleaned up and was able to escape."

Trip really wanted to hear more of this story, but he could tell Daddy was done talking about it.

"But Jimmy's got a lot to lose, right? I mean, you said he's governor of Louisiana . . . ."

"Yep." Daddy cleared his throat again. "Me saving his ass at Dong Hoi kept him alive long enough to become a true hero in the war. After he retired, he parlayed that into ownership of a high-profile private security company that brought him to Hollywood's attention. Ended up playing a few small, memorable movie roles that made him enough of a household name when he decided to enter politics." Daddy cleared his throat. "He's always laid his success at my feet, saying some BS about Dong Hoi being the crucible and me the catalyst."

Unexpected color on his father's cheeks told Trip he was uncomfortable with knowing he was calling in on a debt he never expected to collect. Daddy cleared his throat again and checked his watch.

"It's time."

Trip's heart flipped over in his chest, but he squared his shoulders and compulsively patted the unfamiliar bulk of the HK45 in its shoulder holster. The secondary pistol, a compact HK45, was tucked into a soft holster at the small of his back, along with two extra magazines, fully loaded. The weapons had felt comfortable in his grip when Daddy had gone over them with him, demonstrating the safety mechanisms and explaining the features that made it one of the top choices for military and law enforcement alike.

While he appreciated a reliable weapon as much as any man with a mission, he still sent up a prayer that he wouldn't have to draw either of them.

Then he followed his father into the narrow hall and out through the lobby to the front of the brick-walled motel. They garnered more than a little interest from the guests gathered on the barbeque patio as they waited for the promised car, but they didn't have to wait long.

Apparently, Jimmy was as much a stickler for punctuality as Daddy. Trip only had time to wonder if they should sit to avoid drawing more attention before the white limousine pulled up. The driver, dressed in classic chauffeur attire, ran around to open the door, then closed it behind them once they slid into the dim interior.

chapter
twenty-one

Inside the air-conditioned vehicle, it took Trip a moment to realize there was another man sitting in the back-facing seat. It wasn't until the chauffeur shut the door and ran around to the driver's side that the man drew attention to himself by clearing his throat.

Trip made out the shape of a man large enough to take up most of the bench seat across from them. As his eyes adjusted, he saw the same style of white suit he and his father wore, which stood out even more against the man's black skin. His intense brown eyes scrutinized Trip with calculated precision as the car pulled out onto the street.

"Mission briefing," he said by way of introduction. "The press is covering red carpet arrivals. When it's our turn, the driver will stop beyond the carpet so the governor's vehicle can pull up in the spotlight. A third car with two of my men will be behind it. As the governor's security detail, we'll all exit first. Make a show of scanning for threats. Try not to look like amateurs." The man gave Trip a meaningful look, then nodded to Colton Jr. "With respect, sir. I've heard about what you did for Governor Krause in Vietnam. He has the utmost confidence in your skills, but I also know you've been ranching in Kansas since the war. This here is a thousand miles away from what you've had to deal with lately."

To Trip's surprise, Daddy didn't bristle at the implied insult. He merely grunted. "I know what I don't know, son."

The man nodded again and leaned forward. "The governor doesn't usually make a blatant show of force at functions like this, but he does have a reputation as a no-nonsense politician who calls it like he sees it. The justification for you two is a fabricated rumor that one of the candidates may try to do more than buy the governor's endorsement for his replacement. The governor will play it up as much as needed to get Mama Sanci to buy it. You will act as his bodyguards while my men do the real work from the shadows. We don't expect trouble, but Governor Krause never attends a public function without a security detail, so this is nothing too far out of the ordinary. Stay close to him, but not on top of him. For the entrance, the boy should walk a few paces ahead while you, sir, walk a few paces behind. Be aware he's going to be shaking hands and such, so don't get too far ahead of him. Oh, and take these."

He held out a tiny ear bud to each of them, with curled tubes connected to black wires ending with a small black radio. Daddy took his, and Trip hesitantly accepted his.

The man gave a heavy sigh and showed Trip how to settle the tube around his ear, uncoiling the black wire so it ran down to the neck of his suit where it clipped onto his collar, then along his shoulder before dropping the radio unit into the breast pocket of his suit.

"This is the button you'll push if you need to talk to one of us. We'll thank you not to use it unless it's a true emergency, but the governor wants you two to look official.

Plus, it's conceivable we may need to give you instructions. I understand you're armed?" The question was directed at his father, who nodded. "Then I'll remind you firing a weapon in a room full of people has consequences, especially the quality of folk attending tonight. I recommend avoiding that scenario at all costs." The man looked at Trip, and he didn't miss the derision dripping from his tone.

Trip bit back the urge to tell this guy he wasn't a complete back-country hick—that he wouldn't do anything stupid—then realized he really was a liability. Even if nothing happened and he only had to follow Governor Krause around a glamorous party, this was still a world away from anything he'd experienced in his life thus far.

In a moment of clarity, he decided the way the man was treating him was designed to tick him off, make him mad so he'd get out of his head and out of his fear—and it had worked. For the six seconds he'd been mad enough to spit, he hadn't been thinking about the likelihood that this was more than he could handle.

He channeled that focus with the discipline his daddy had taught him and kept his mind on the game.

"How will we find Savannah? What if she's not at the party?"

The man gave him a pleased look, as though acknowledging his mental shift. "The governor is going to play hard to get, but Mama Sanci has been trying to get him alone for months. Tonight he plans to let her coax him to her home to talk shop. If the daughter isn't at the Roosevelt for the event, she will most certainly be at the mansion. Chances are good you'll be able to slip away to search for her. The downside is she's not likely to let the entire security detail come inside. We'll have to play it by ear."

Trip nodded, trying to think of more questions, trying to get in the headspace of someone whose job was to spot potential problems before they start, but he was interrupted when the man leaned forward again.

"My code name is Pitbull, by the way."

Daddy blinked at him. "Sorry?"

"On the radio. My code name is Pitbull. Either of you have a preference? Should I just pick something from a comic movie? I heard they called you Pale Rider in the jungle, sir."

Daddy shook his head. "Just call me Junior, son. That's code enough for me."

Pitbull turned to Trip. "You?"

The only thing that came to mind was the nickname Savannah had given him the night they'd played poker into the wee hours. "Ace, I guess."

"That'll do," Pitbull said.

Through the earpiece, Trip heard a confident voice say they were one minute from arrival. He turned to look out the tinted window as they rolled up to the Roosevelt Hotel's entryway.

The front of the hotel was so understated, if it hadn't been for the hordes of reporters gathered in clusters by the steps, he would have looked right past the framed, chocolate-brown awning. But white lettering declared, "Roosevelt - A Waldorf Astoria Hotel." Even he knew Waldorf Astoria was a big deal. Two runners of literal red carpet ran down the steps all the way to the curb, where men in black suits and valets in fancy uniforms held the crowd at bay.

As Pitbull had described, they pulled up past the steps, then exited the vehicle. Trip did his best to impersonate James Bond as he raked his gaze over the crowd, looking for trouble. He followed Pitbull's lead and moved toward the steps, holding his hand out as if to ward off any eager photographers. Head on a swivel, he scanned the crowd, hoping against hope to catch sight of Savannah. The flashing of cameras and press of reporters with microphones let him know the governor was approaching. He glanced back to see the man from the truck stop dressed in an immaculate steel-gray suit, a brilliant smile gracing a face that defied age. That was all Trip had time to register about the man before he had to return to his duty.

After what seemed like ages of the governor "gladhanding" the crowd and placating the press with neat soundbites, they reached the top of the stairs and passed through the wood-framed glass doors into the stunning lobby. Through the press of bodies, Trip caught glimpses of marble floors and sections of intricately designed mosaic tiles, huge pillars with gold accents, giant potted palm trees—and more people. These folks were all elegantly dressed, sparkling with jewels and gold watches, honest-to-goodness cufflinks on the men, crystal flutes of champagne in hands, and a general hum of conversation and tittering laughter.

The governor paused after making his entry, putting a hand on Trip's elbow. His voice came low to Trip's ear. "Easy now, lad. Follow my lead and stay about two feet behind me. You're doing fine."

Trip wasn't sure how he hadn't lost his composure yet, but the governor's words were just what he needed to hear. He held it together as Governor Krause made more greetings and idle conversation with the New Orleans elite, making his way toward the center of the room. Just as he thought he might be able to settle into the role, a raised voice called out the governor's name.

chapter
twenty-two

"Bonswa, Governor Krause!" The sing-song lilt that was similar yet oh-so-different from Savannah's belonged to a petite figure dressed in an elegant silk pantsuit of pristine white fabric that set off against skin matching Savannah's golden-brown hue. As she glided toward the governor, Trip noted the similarities and differences and his breath caught in his throat. If the mother was so close, where was Savannah?

"Mama Sanci," Governor Krause said, his tone warm but not as sickly sweet as the woman's. "You look lovely, as always."

Her laughter was loud and about as real as a snake clucking like a chicken. Trip struggled to keep his expression neutral. "You are too kind, James. May I call you James?" She swept on without waiting for his answer, her hand on his forearm with a familiarity that caused the governor to stiffen. "I'm so glad you agreed to come tonight, *shær*. I truly was not expecting it."

Trip found himself reacting to the governor's demeanor by taking a step toward them, and the woman called Mama Sanci looked at him in surprise. Before he could say or do any more, Pitbull was at Trip's side, murmuring something in his ear about taking it easy before moving toward the governor, whispering in his ear as well. Governor Krause nodded, and Pitbull faded back into the crowd.

"Who are these gentlemen?" Mama Sanci's expression when she'd looked at Pitbull had been tainted by a kind of revulsion Trip didn't understand, along with some not-so-veiled venom. When her gaze shifted to Trip, her attitude visibly softened, though not by much.

"My security detail," the governor said. "Hadn't you heard? There've been rumors of a threat against me."

"Shocking," she said, with about as much emotion as a card shark. Trip wondered if the so-called rumors weren't based on more truth than Pitbull had let on. Then she laughed her big, fake laugh again. "But of course you are safe in my company, *shær*. I don't want it to be said our beloved governor was harmed at my soiree."

She continued speaking, but Trip lost track of her words when he caught sight of Savannah moving through the crowd toward them. At least, it looked like Savannah on the surface. Same skin tone of a warm field of wheat at sunset, same sinfully curvaceous body filling out a deadly red satin dress, but her eyes were not the lively green he remembered. This version of Savannah was lifeless by comparison. Trip's heart went out to her as he theorized how thoroughly demoralized she must feel at being back under her mother's control.

Then he noticed the man beside her guiding her by the elbow, drawing her to a stop beside her mother. There was an air about the man that suggested he was in law enforcement, or maybe Mama Sanci's own security detail. He looked for the tell-tale sign of an earpiece or perhaps the bulge of a weapon at the man's waist. Before he could confirm his suspicions, the man whispered in Savannah's ear, and she spoke almost simultaneously.

"*Moman*, the banquet room is ready." It was not Savannah's voice, rather a flat parody of the saucy tone she'd often taken when speaking to him. Her gaze never even flickered toward him—not that he had any reason to think she'd recognize him given his uncharacteristic costume.

"Ah, Savannah!" the woman fairly purred as she pulled Savannah close to her side, her grip on Savannah's upper arm tight. "Governor Krause, have you met my daughter? She's just returned from a sojourn in the Mediterranean."

"I don't believe I've had the pleasure," the governor said, extending his hand. Savannah reached out slowly, as if on autopilot, and he took her hand, bending over it to kiss it in old-fashioned courtesy.

She made no reaction, just blinked slowly, until her mother jostled her arm. "It's a pleasure to meet you," she said, her voice slurred just a tad. Had she been drinking?

Mama Sanci laughed again, pulling her daughter against her side in a kind of half-hug. "She just arrived this morning. The *pòv shær* is still jet-lagged. But Savannah was just so determined to be here to support me. Weren't you, *shær*?"

She gave her another little shake that would have appeared affectionate, except Savannah just seemed to endure it. There was no answering affection. She didn't even look at her mother as she responded in a dull tone. "Yes, *Moman*. I am very tired, but I wanted to hear your speech."

Mama Sanci smiled indulgently before handing her off to the man who had brought her to the group. The two moved with the crowd toward a set of double doors that let into the large room Trip could see beyond. Apparently this was the banquet room where the gubernatorial candidate was going to make her speech.

Governor Krause leaned toward Mama Sanci, but not so close Trip couldn't hear his remark. "You never told me she was such a beauty."

"Oh, you like what you see, James?" Mama Sanci was purring again. "She is a delightful, obedient child, willing to do anything for me. Perhaps you would like her company this evening."

Trip blinked, sure he imagined the emphasis the woman put on the word "anything." Surely she wasn't suggesting . . . . He couldn't conceive of a woman offering up her daughter as a. . . a. . . companion to a man just to try to secure his support. Then again, this was the same woman who had ordered a man killed in front of the same daughter to protect herself from even the slightest scandal. But why would she think Savannah would ever go along with such a scheme?

Governor Krause gave him a look of reassurance even as he answered the woman. "I'm sure she would make a delightful companion. I rather like my. . . ahem. . . companions to be biddable and sweet."

It was all Trip could do not to growl at the governor's blatantly suggestive tone, but he realized it was all part of the setup, designed to get Mama Sanci to invite him to the house. And it was working.

Mama Sanci's chuckle was low and throaty. "I have already arranged for her to be your table companion. Perhaps after the banquet, you will come to *lamézon* for a nightcap. After we have had a chance to speak of business, the night's pleasures can resume."

Rather than answer, Governor Krause simply inclined his head with a small smile.

Mama Sanci patted his hand and gave him a wink before turning to follow Savannah into the banquet hall.

SAVANNAH SLOWLY EMERGED FROM A DEEP, deep fog. Threads of conversations, blurred faces drifting in and out of view, a voice whispering in her ear, prompting her to speak, but she held no recollection of the words. A vague nagging in the back of her mind suggested she should be angry, or terrified, or resisting whatever was going on around her at the very least, but she couldn't summon the energy to delve deeper and act on it. She ought to struggle harder, the voice whispered, but try as she might, she couldn't grasp what was going on around her.

Her feet moved, the blurs swayed in her vision, the sound of distant conversations swelled and faded, her own voice sounded dead in her ears. Time passed. Then she realized she was sitting in a chair, a cool stem of crystal balanced in her fingers, and her eyes began to focus at last on a plate of food in front of her. On autopilot, she raised the champagne flute to her lips.

A familiar, frightening voice sounded over the sound system, and her fingers fumbled the glass. It almost fell from her grip, but someone reached over her shoulder and caught it before even a drop could spill. She looked up into eyes so blue she felt herself diving into them, drowning in them, until all she could do was stare.

"I've got you." That voice. That voice was a lifeline, and she clung to it. "Are you all right, ma'am?"

Something was wrong, horribly wrong. That voice was familiar to her, why would he speak as though she were a stranger? Then those eyes moved back, and she saw another pair of eyes watching her—and these were cold and calculating, terrifying.

"*Mo chagrin*, I'm sorry. I am jet-lagged," she heard herself saying, words programmed into her over the last several hours. The kind, blue-eyed man stepped back from her, and she frowned as her thoughts finally began to coalesce. There had been a job in a small town where she'd felt safe for a time. And a man . . . . The thought of him quickened her heartbeat. Then she'd suffered a ride in a truck with two men who took turns leering at her while the other drove. She'd emerged blinking into the sun, only to be pushed into a car with heavily tinted windows. She'd managed to see road signs for Denver, then Englewood, and then a red stone pillar with the words Centennial Airport. A swift exchange into a plane on the tarmac of the private airfield, and she was winging away with the sun behind them, heading east.

East.

In mere hours she stood before her mother, enduring disdain and smug triumph in eyes she had hoped never to see again. There had been no speeches, no recrimination, nothing but the sting of a needle in her arm before the world went fuzzy and gray. Nothing beyond that was remotely clear. Questions about where she had been, who she had spoken to. Lying, lying, lying that she had just been hiding in a hotel. Tears of fear and begging for forgiveness. Begging for mercy. Hours of a voice droning instructions at her. Weaving a story until she almost believed it was truth. *Spent the summer in Greece with friends, enjoyed my time but wanted to come home to support* Moman *in her campaign. Arrived just this morning. Jet lag. Isn't the weather in New Orleans fine this time of year?*

Raising her hand, Savannah put two fingers to her forehead and pressed as her mother's voice continued about bringing Louisiana into the future. Making it great again. She couldn't focus on the words, only on the growing realization of where she was and that voice telling her "I've got you" giving her hope. In the process of turning to look behind her, she caught sight of a familiar face and froze.

Laurencett. She couldn't help but cringe as he reached out and patted her hand. "Are you feeling all right, Savannah?" he asked in a low voice, leaning in close. "Have a sip of my whiskey. You'll feel better."

He passed her his glass, helping her take a long, slow pull of the fiery liquid that burned all the way to her gut. Almost immediately, she felt the world shift into the fog again. Her eyes widened at the implication that he had put something in his own drink so as not to get caught slipping something into hers.

That was her last coherent thought before everything devolved into the haziness of nightmare.

Trip bristled as the man sitting beside Savannah leaned in and spoke into her ear. He overheard the questioning concern for her health, saw him offer her a sip of his drink. He wanted to slap the glass away from her lips—he'd been careful to watch *her* drink against someone tampering with it but hadn't thought to watch her table companion with his own drink.

He'd been hopeful when he'd made eye contact with her moments earlier, thought he'd seen a flicker of recognition in her eyes, but now she was swaying again, fingers fumbling as she clutched the man's suit jacket.

The man folded her into the crook of his arm, nestling

her head against his shoulder as Mama Sanci began to wrap up her speech.

"The poor dear," he said, looking over at Governor Krause. "She's exhausted. I promised her mother I'd look out for her."

"And you are?" the governor asked coolly before taking a sip of his own champagne.

"A family friend. Emmanuel Laurencett," he said, offering his free hand for the governor to shake. "Savannah is like the little sister I never had." He turned his head to look down at Savannah, his expression anything but that of a doting brother.

"Ah," the governor said. "I do hope she recovers enough to keep me company later this evening."

Before Laurencett could respond, or Trip could shudder at the airs the governor was adopting, Mama Sanci called out for the crowd to support her in her bid for governor. Everyone rose to their feet, clapping with enthusiasm. Governor Krause stood as well, clapping politely, while Laurencett pulled Savannah to her feet and began guiding her out a side door. Trip was ready to follow, but Jimmy put a hand on his sleeve.

"Patience," he said.

chapter
twenty-three

"Lord-a-mighty, Junior, but it's a helluva thing to have you on my team again." There was more of a twang in the governor's voice, and Trip realized these were the first words he'd exchanged with Daddy that weren't part of the ruse.

"Though this," the governor waved his hand to indicate the posh limo they had all just crammed themselves into for the ride over to Mama Sanci's home, ". . . we never dreamed of an assignment like this in the jungle."

The fierce, wolfish grin his father gave was like nothing Trip had ever seen, reminding him there was a whole side to his father Trip would never know. "No sir, Sarge."

"Well, to be fair, survival occupied much of my attention over there."

Trip thought for a moment the man was going to launch into the story of how Daddy had saved his life in Vietnam. As much as he wanted to hear a different recounting of the story—sure to be hair-raising given the governor's willingness to go out of his way to help—Trip wanted more to focus on Savannah.

Thankfully, the man knew when it was time to stay on point.

"Right. Pitbull can give us the recon intel he was able to gather in the last twenty-four hours…."

As the men now began discussing things in technical terms, Trip found it hard to concentrate on the words. Seeing Savannah Dawn again had been a jolt to his system. Though it hadn't been very long time-wise, it felt like ages. Seeing the barest flicker of recognition in her eyes had given him heart, but she'd been so changed from the woman he'd come to know, he felt a strip had torn out of his soul.

What had they done to her in such a short period of time?

When he'd reached to steady her hand, his fingers had grazed hers, sending a spark of. . . something. . . through him. Not desire. How messed up would it be to think of sex at a time like this? No. The feeling was one of "rightness." Being near her was important to him, to his sense of being a man. . . a complete man. Or a man whose life felt complete because Savannah was in it.

But now was not the time to fixate on what should be. The reality was the woman who'd stolen his heart while he wasn't looking needed him to be on his A Game. She needed his focus on the matter at hand, which was to free her from her mother's clutches.

"Pay attention, son." His father's words were not unkind, but they were firm enough to snap Trip's attention back to the moment.

"Sorry, sir," he said, turning away from the view of St. Charles Street with its streetcars passing outside the window of the limousine.

"Mama Sanci's mansion is one of the oldest in the

Garden District," Pitbull said. "As such, it has a lot of rooms. It's impossible to know which one Savannah might be in. She might even be housed in the old servant's quarters—a separate building on the other side of the driveway. They'd be able to have a guard on her there without drawing too much attention to that fact."

"We need to be sure she's brought to us," Governor Krause said. "I'll be playing up the mayor's suggestion that I spend time with her daughter as an incentive to garner my support. I need to be sure you don't react to anything I say, Trip. I know you love her, but showing yourself as the protective boyfriend won't serve to help her now."

Trip blinked. Love? Is that what he was feeling? The governor went on before Trip could analyze that notion further.

"So keep your head in the game. Do you think you can do that? We can keep you on door duty if you'd rather."

"No, sir. I can do it. I'll do anything to help her—including keeping up my poker face. As far as anyone there is concerned, I'm just here for your safety."

"Good man," Governor Krause said. "Now, if she's there for the meeting, I'm ready to say whatever's needed to make Mama Sanci believe I will support her bid for governor—especially if she gives me some alone time with Savannah. I'll do my best to get her out into the garden. Alone. Pitbull will be ready to extract her via the back garden wall."

"Our recon didn't show a gate," Pitbull broke in, "but we should be able to get her over the wall if we have a few minutes to spare."

"I'll deal with the fallout of going back inside without her," the governor went on. "It's likely to be FUBAR, but I don't think she'll risk trying to harm me. I made sure certain contacts of mine know I'm coming here, and I made sure she heard me do it, so she'll be careful. With luck, someone will be at her gate with cameras rolling to document my arrival and, ideally, my safe departure."

All this talk of the governor's safety was irritating to Trip. How could the man be making this all about him? His life wasn't the one at risk. Was it?

Except. . . if Savannah's mother really was as unhinged as Savannah had said, perhaps the risk to Governor Krause was real. If Mama Sanci thought she had everything to lose with Savannah's renewed defection, what wouldn't she do to keep her under wraps?

Still, for Trip, Savannah's safety was priority one. The governor could surely take care of himself.

"What if that woman decides to play coy with you, draw it out? What if Savannah isn't allowed to attend? How do we find her?"

"We didn't have time to arrange for any of the good high-tech gear," Pitbull said. "So, no tracking by transponders, heat signatures, or the like. It will have to be an old-fashioned room-by-room search. One of you will have to devise an excuse to get away from the group, search the house, and when you find her, get her outside. Depending on where you end up, we'll figure out how to extract you both."

Trip was sure there was more to plan, but they were out of time. The car pulled up in front of a wrought iron gate in a brick wall overgrown by ivy. Trip watched as the car bearing Savannah and her mother passed through the gate ahead of them, then they pulled through, up the driveway and in between two buildings.

To steady his nerves, Trip studied the mayor's estate.

The building on the right was the smaller of the two.

Two-stories and painted white, it lacked the columns that marked the main house as the focus of the visitor's attention. He dismissed it from consideration as soon as it became clear Savannah wasn't going into it.

The plantation-style house wasn't as big as Trip expected, but it was certainly grand on a scale he hadn't seen before. It oozed money, from the ornate scrollwork on the columns to the wrought iron railings of balconies. Even the well-tamed landscape spoke of an army of gardeners.

This place belonged to someone rich and influential, and the sight of it set Trip's teeth on edge with the knowledge they weren't up against an average opponent with no means to back their efforts.

Trip was first to slide out of the seat and through the limo's door into the cooling night air. Pausing to scan his surroundings, he forced his gaze to slide past where Savannah was being ushered into the house. All he wanted was to run to her.

After a beat, he stepped aside so his father and the governor could exit the vehicle in turn. Pitbull stayed inside.

Governor Krause stopped by the driver's door, and the window rolled down.

"That will be all for now, Anthony. I'll text you when I'm ready to leave." He ran a finger along the roof of the car. "It's looking a bit dusty. Why don't you take it to get washed?"

"Very good, sir," Anthony replied.

The exchange was all for show—voices loud enough to be overheard by the staff at the mansion's door, and only an excuse to get the car and Pitbull back out through the gate.

For Trip, the next moments passed in a blur. The old

mansion was not only opulent on the outside, but inside as well. Paintings on the walls of men and women dressed in classic Southern attire, many in gilded frames, looked like something out of that mini-series about the Civil War by that long-winded author, James somebody. There were crystal chandeliers, expensive vases, statuettes. . . and all this just in the entry foyer.

The household staff escorted them through the house and out onto a garden patio—one with a clear view across the manicured lawn beyond stone cherubim playing in a vast fountain and out to the wall.

So much for Plan A of getting Savannah alone in the garden.

Mama Sanci was already settled onto a wicker couch, Savannah by her side. A butler gestured for Governor Krause to sit in a matching wicker chair across the veranda from her.

It was an intimate space, especially given the grand spaces of the rest of the mansion. A circular coffee table was all that separated the two politicians, and as they settled into small talk, Trip and his father took up positions a discreet distance from either end of the chair.

Trip followed his father's lead as he stood with his hands clasped behind his back, like a soldier at parade rest.

Trip tried to focus on his "job," to stay attentive to his surroundings, but he could feel Savannah's eyes on him even when he wasn't looking her way.

SAVANNAH'S AWARENESS swam to the surface as though she were waking from a deep sleep. Again. She had the sense that time had passed, but she wasn't sure how long. She was in a different location, too. Familiar, though. The garden patio of the place she'd called home for most of her life.

Her mother was talking about her campaign, discussing the finer points of reaching voters through radio and television ads. Then a man encouraged her to star in her own ads—let the people see her face, hear her voice. His earnest inflection drew her gaze, and she recognized him. Governor James Krause.

He was here because her mother needed his support.

Moman had made him a promise. Promised him time with her daughter. The memory squeezed Savannah's soul. Her mother was pimping her out to further her campaign. Through the haze still clinging to her thoughts, she cringed at the knowledge she was little more than a tool to her mother—a means to an end.

A subtle movement to the governor's left drew her attention, and she took note of the man standing near the end of the couch. Once she saw him, she couldn't look away.

His broad-shouldered frame was familiar. When he turned his gaze on her, she recognized the kind eyes of the man from the banquet. But there was more recognition than that. She'd spent time with him. Laughed with him. Looked into those eyes. Kissed him . . . .

The memory encouraged her as much as it confused her. Who was this man? Why did she associate him with food, with wide open spaces. . . with freedom?

Before these flashes could consolidate into something she could hold onto, her mother nudged her with her elbow.

"*Obeyi mwen*, child. The governor wants to see you in something pretty, *petit mwen*. Let's not disappoint him, *wi?*"

Albert was at her elbow, urging her to rise, and she

dutifully did as *Moman* had requested. She had no choice. Of all the memories she could put her mind to, that one rose above them all. *Moman* always got what she wanted.

Resistance may have bought her some time, but ultimately it had been futile.

chapter
twenty-four

T rip caught himself from taking more than a half-step forward when the butler helped Savannah to her feet and he and a woman dressed in a traditional maid's uniform ushered her from the room. He yearned to follow them, see where they were taking her, but he resisted. The governor was giving him no indication of taking action, and his father had given an almost imperceptible shake of his head.

"Is she all right?" Jimmy asked, but Trip heard a sick kind of lecherous curiosity, as if it wouldn't matter one way or another.

"She's tired," Mama Sanci said. "But she'll do as she's told, whatever is asked of her."

Jimmy smiled in approval. "Excellent," he said. "My wife is a strong woman, which is well and good—and plays well to the female voters, by the way—but for recreational purposes, I like a woman who does as she's told."

Mama Sanci's eyes glittered. "Then you should enjoy Savannah's. . . company. She's a very good girl."

Trip had to swallow down the bile rising in his throat.

If he'd had any doubt Savannah's mother was a monster, this exchange removed it.

To his surprise, Jimmy turned to his father. "Why don't you boys retire to the kitchen, have one of those sweet little maids get you some iced tea. I don't think I have anything to worry about from Mama Sanci."

"Sir," his father said without hesitation, then moved toward the door to the house.

"Sir," Trip echoed, following. It was the perfect excuse to get inside to search for Savannah. . . except the man called Laurencett followed them.

That was problematic. Trip was sure he and his father could convince the maid and butler to show them around or let them wander, but. . . an FBI agent? One who may or may not already have a notion they were not who they claimed to be? After all, FBI agents were trained to spot threats in unlikely suspects, weren't they? Trip had to assume the man was onto them, and he tried desperately to think of a way to evade him.

They entered the sprawling kitchen behind the maid. The butler collected a tray with a crystal decanter and two matching crystal tumblers from the sideboard, then immediately took his leave back outside.

The maid busied herself fixing up two glasses of iced tea, while Laurencett helped himself to a crystal tumbler of his own, which he filled with a generous portion of whiskey.

"Do you like your tea sweet?" the maid asked, her voice thick with a drawl that was both similar yet different from Savannah's. It lacked the exotic sound of the Creole accent.

"Unsweetened, I'm guessing," Laurencett answered for them. "They're working men. Fit and lean. I'm willing to bet neither of them have a sweet tooth. Nor are they tempted by bourbon, I'd say." He raised his glass in salute.

Daddy grunted his agreement, but Trip was tempted to ask for sugar, just to wipe that smug look off the man's face. He realized in time it was such a small thing, letting the agent be right was more likely to put him at ease than trying to prove him wrong.

"Just tea for me," he said instead, then accepted the glass from the pretty girl, who smiled shyly up at him.

"New to the job, are you?" Laurencett asked, leaning against the sideboard and sipping at his glass.

Trip felt panic rise in his belly. Did they have a cover story? He couldn't remember. This was exactly why he hadn't wanted to stray too far from the truth. What if he said the wrong thing?

Daddy came to the rescue. "More or less. You?"

The agent gave him a long look over the rim of his glass as he took another sip. "Long time. Over twenty years. I can spot rookies a mile away." He paused a beat. "You're pretty old to be a rookie."

Daddy didn't even blink, just lifted a shoulder in a half-shrug. "Money's tight. Need the extra cash. Army recruiter didn't lie when he said I'd always be able to fall back on my military training." Daddy took a sip of his tea before continuing. "Never thought I'd need it at my age, truth to tell. It's just right. Thank you, darlin'," he added, lifting his glass to the maid.

She dipped a curtsey, then turned back to the refrigerator to pull out a tray of deviled eggs, which she took outside.

Laurencett didn't move. "What about you?" he asked, turning to Trip. "You're so green I bet your code name is Kermit."

Trip bristled. "Green or not, I can bench press two of

you." Laurencett didn't even blink, which told Trip he'd been expecting a reply like that, so he added under his breath, "Pound you into the ground like a fencepost, jackass."

That made the agent laugh uneasily, as if he knew it were true. "Easy, big guy. I don't doubt your qualifications. Just making an observation. Everybody's gotta start somewhere. Father and son, if I'm not mistaken. And not from around here."

Trip couldn't help it. He stilled at the implication this agent had figured them out. Realized their accents had given them away. But how much had Laurencett really figured out? How much was he bluffing?

It really was a bit like poker, wasn't it? The "cards" were small truths and small lies. Winning the "hand" was determined by who could read the other player better. And the stakes. . . well, the stakes were higher than any game Trip had played.

"My father is a hero. What son wouldn't want to follow wherever he led?" Trip found himself saying. "When he found work for both of us in personal security, I jumped at the chance to follow him—at the chance to make him proud."

He dared a look at his father, letting the mixture of chagrin and pride he felt for his old man show on his face. There was more truth than lie in his statement, and he wanted Laurencett to focus in on the truth while still absorbing the lie.

Treating the situation like a poker game felt like a stroke of brilliance. Trip was good at poker. Even his own brother couldn't read him to know what cards he held. He could bluff this FBI agent too.

Couldn't he?

LAURENCETT FLICKED his gaze to the old man. He didn't buy it. A couple good old boys from the Midwest just decided to become bodyguards for the governor of Louisiana? Not likely. But he kept his thoughts to himself. No sense in letting on that he knew something was up.

That sly minx had somehow found champions in that tiny berg in Kansas. He was sure of it. How they'd made it here so quickly was a mystery. Clearly the truck drivers had been seen. . . or Savannah had told these cowboys her story. They'd not bother to search for a kidnap victim, opting instead to just go straight to the only place that made sense—if they knew the whole story.

He cursed inwardly. These two were a complication he didn't need. Mama Sanci would expect him to take care of them. No doubt the governor would need to be dealt with too.

Things had just gotten very messy in a very short period of time.

He'd have trouble dealing with these two men by himself, so he'd have to set them at ease, get them to let their guard down.

"I get it," he said in response to the younger man's declaration. "My dad was a world-class screw up, but I always dreamed I'd have someone to look up to, whose footsteps I'd be proud to walk in. Must be nice to work together too."

"It has its challenges," the old man said, at the same time his son said, "We have our moments."

Laurencett laughed in appreciation of their words, playing up to their sense of security. Then he pulled out his phone with an apologetic smile.

"Please excuse me. When I work late, my four-year-old expects me to call and wish her goodnight at bedtime. I'll just be a moment." He headed into the foyer, dialing Guidry and putting the phone to his ear while the men in the kitchen were still in earshot. "Sorry to keep you waiting, pumpkin," he said before the call even connected. "Do you have Mr. Fluffers all tucked in?"

By the time Guidry picked up, he was around the corner.

"Yeah, boss?"

"I need you and three of your most trusted here in fifteen minutes or less," he said, cupping his hand over the microphone and pitching his voice low. "We have a delicate situation."

He hung up. Guidry would not let him down. Guidry was paid enough to guarantee he would be on call twenty-four/seven.

As Emmanuel came back around the corner, he cooed into the phone, "Daddy loves you, baby. Big loves and kisses." He smacked his lips in the kind of exaggerated kissing sound men regularly made fools of themselves with when it came to their daughters. He didn't have kids, and didn't plan on ever settling down, but portraying a doting father would set these men at ease.

"My apologies, gentlemen. My little angel gets particularly devilish if she doesn't get her goodnight loves on time. Do you have any children?" he asked the younger man, steering the conversation to the most innocuous subject he could think of.

TRIP RESISTED the urge to look at his watch as he tried to figure out how long Savannah had been away supposedly changing clothes. The FBI agent had been yammering on about children for forever, and Trip was beginning to worry he wouldn't have a chance to search for her while she was away from the others. Once she came back, surely the odds of freeing her tonight would go down significantly.

"I've got to use the head," his father said abruptly. "Which way?"

It was a brilliant solution to their problem. If Laurencett simply gave directions, Daddy could slip off and search for Savannah. If he escorted him, Trip could do the searching.

The agent's hesitation was so brief Trip almost missed it, but the man cheerfully held out a hand to indicate Daddy should precede him through a doorway off the kitchen.

The second the man disappeared from view, Trip darted out a door on the opposite side of the room, tiptoeing to keep the stiff heels of his dress shoes from striking the hardwood floors.

Once in the foyer, he dashed to the stairs leading up to the second story and hurried up as quietly as possible. Hallways stretched out in either direction. Before he could wonder which way to go, he saw a man standing outside a door close by.

At Trip's abrupt arrival the man turned, a look of mistrust plain on his face.

"What are you doing up here?" he said coldly. "Guests are not allowed on the residents' floor."

"I'm sorry," Trip said, trying to think fast. "I really gotta go and someone is using the bathroom downstairs." He continued toward the man, debating whether he should shuffle like a three-year-old doing the pee-pee dance. "Which way?"

The man scowled. "There's more than one restroom downstairs, mister. Kindly turn around . . . ." He put his hand out to point back the way Trip had come, and Trip grabbed it, yanking him forward into his upraised knee. When the man doubled over, he followed up with a two-handed blow to the back of the man's head—a blow he imagined to be like the one that had felled him back in Syracuse.

Trip caught him as the man went down, settling him as gently as possible to the floor, just as Pitbull's voice came over the headset to whisper in his ear, "We've got company."

The realization Trip had been issued a two-way radio struck him as soon as he thought he should update the team on his situation. But what did he have to report, really? He stood indecisively in the hall for a split second before he made for the door the man had been guarding.

He gently tried the handle, relieved when the knob turned freely. Easing the door open, he peered around the edge, hoping to get the lay of the room and see if Savannah was there—and if she was alone.

The door was more than halfway open before he saw her standing in front of a full-length mirror wearing a white, lacy night-dress and matching sheer dressing gown.

Good grief, her mother was shameless. How could she even pretend this getup was acceptable attire for entertaining a guest?

Trip stepped into the room, his eyes glued to Savannah, who stood staring blankly at her own reflection.

"Miss Dawn," he breathed, but got no farther before he felt the cold steel of a gun barrel against the back of his head.

"Stop right there, Romeo," a woman's voice said. Trip froze, slowly raising his hands in surrender.

"I can see the wheels turning in your mind, and don't think that just because I'm a woman you can get the drop on me. I will end you in a heartbeat."

It sounded like a line out of some cheesy spy movie, but Trip didn't think it would be wise to test the woman's skill or resolve. For all he knew, she really was a capable spy. After all, Mama Sanci had at least one FBI agent in her pocket, why not two?

"You got me," he said, beginning to turn toward the woman. Before he could see who was there, a foot struck him in the back of his knee, and rough hands pushed him face-first into the floor.

"Use these to tie his hands," the woman said, and Trip realized the guard from the hall must not have stayed unconscious very long.

Some kind of cord wrapped around his wrists while a knee pressed between his shoulder blades. He heard a sound like a woman whimpering, then pain exploded in his head right before everything went dark.

chapter
twenty-five

It was a nightmare. Savannah had almost convinced herself. The kind man she was finally remembering to be Trip—Colton Thomas the Third—from the ranch in Kansas had somehow come through her bedroom door, but Bethany, who had been there making sure she obeyed her mother's orders, had pulled a gun on him. Then another man had come in and pushed him to the floor before striking him on the back of his head.

She'd cried out, only to have the woman turn the gun on her.

"Quiet, girl. There're worse things than being shot. Right, Max?" At that, the man leered up at her. He didn't need to say anything for her to realize what those "worse things" might be.

"But *Moman* . . . ," she tried.

"Your mother authorized whatever means necessary to ensure your cooperation. You gave up the easy way when you fled."

Savannah's shoulders sagged in defeat. The woman might be bluffing, but if Bethany thought she was getting bold, she would give her another shot of whatever it was that turned her into a high-functioning sleepwalker—one fully susceptible to suggestion. And Savannah had only just begun to find her way back into her own mind, her own memories, her own will. She was aware enough to know she had to pretend to go along with those who held power over her. It was no longer just her life on the line.

She didn't know how Trip had come to be in her home —in her room!—and while it terrified her for his sake, it gave her heart. Surely he wouldn't have come without a plan. Without backup. Surely he wasn't alone.

"Yes," she whispered. "Of course."

"Come to me," Bethany commanded, the look in her eye suggesting she was testing Savannah's compliance. Savannah moved without hesitation, though not too quickly, and stood facing Bethany, ready for her next command.

After looking her in the eye for an uncomfortably long minute, Bethany then looked her up and down, inspecting her appearance.

"If we're going to pull this off . . . ," something in her voice said she wasn't speaking to either of the people in the room, "we have to convince the governor his bodyguards were plotting against him. And we need her to distract him."

She paused a moment. Then, "Well, if he doesn't buy it, we move on to the terminal option." Another pause. "I know it's risky, but what else can we do? Yeah, I thought not. We'll be down in a moment. Be ready."

Bethany's grip on her elbow was tight and insistent as she propelled Savannah to the door. She didn't dare look down at Trip for fear she'd give away her own state of mind. She had to pretend she was still a walking zombie while she figured out what, if anything, she could do to save Trip. She had no doubt he would be killed "resisting arrest" if she couldn't figure a way out of this mess.

PAIN WOKE Trip with the fire of nerves pinching and muscles pulling as his arms—pinned behind his back— were raised and he was dragged to his feet. Flexing his arms helped ease the strain, and he lifted his head as he stood fully upright. He had to blink to be sure his eyes were open, but there was little difference between open and closed. When someone pushed him from behind, he felt the flutter of fabric against his face and realized a hood of some sort was over his head.

"What's going on?" he said, and only received a thump on the back of his head in response.

He staggered forward after another push threatened to send him sprawling. Then, constant pressure against his back let him know he was supposed to keep walking. He tried shuffling his feet, feeling his way forward, but the pressure was too insistent. He bit back a grunt as his shoulder struck something solid. A doorframe?

Then his foot was out over air and he felt himself falling forward. He pitched himself backward out of instinct. His heel slipped off the lip of what must have been the staircase and he fell, tailbone striking a hard edge. The blow sent a shock through his entire body, then another as he skidded down the next step, and the next. His captors weren't being very careful with him. Through his pain he thought perhaps they'd hoped he'd fall and break his neck. After three or four treads, he caught himself and stood on shaky feet.

"Keep moving or we'll send you down on your head."

It was the voice of the woman with the gun. How much earlier had that been? He had no idea.

He wondered how his father was doing. Had he been caught out? Was he still roaming free, or was he trussed up like a Christmas turkey too? What about the governor? Pitbull? Could he expect to be extracted from this mess? Or had it gotten even bigger?

And where was Savannah in all this? Was she safe, or had he ruined whatever apparent truce she'd had with her mother with his botched rescue attempt?

At the bottom of the stairs, hands spun him around in circles a couple times, until he was well and truly disoriented. When they pushed him in the back, he didn't know if he was walking out the front door, back to the garden, into the kitchen, or into some completely unknown part of the house.

They were taking very effective steps to keep him off-center. He could do nothing but follow their cues, and it was infuriating.

COLTON CURSED as he tested the bathroom door only to find it locked from the outside. That alone spoke volumes about this household. Who had locks that kept people *in* bathrooms? There was no window, no way out except breaking down the door.

It had been a gamble, using the bathroom diversion, but he'd gotten the sense the FBI agent was onto them. He hoped Trip had taken the initiative and gone out to search when the man left the kitchen.

Colton had taken his time, trying to delay a return to

the kitchen, when Trip would surely be discovered missing. But this locked door was a bad sign.

He knocked on the door and, in an effort to maintain the charade, called out, "Hello? Door seems to be stuck!"

He heard nothing from the other side of the door, but through his earpiece, he heard Pitbull's report from his position outside: "We've got company."

Then the sound of a scuffle from upstairs.

"Son of a . . . ." He backed up to get a run at the door. It swung open just before he struck it, and he found himself crashing into the wall across the hall from the bathroom door. When he turned, he found himself face to face with the barrel of a pistol.

It was hard to make himself see beyond the weapon to the man holding it. Adrenaline spiked through him to narrow his focus, and he forced himself to take several deep breaths to overcome the fight-or-flight instinct trying to take over.

"What's going on?" he asked as he put his hands in the air in surrender. "I thought the door was stuck . . . ."

"Come now," Laurencett said. "Don't think you can play me for a fool. I know you and the boy are here on some kind of rescue mission. A fool's mission. By yourself, you might have pulled off that cover story, but the boy failed to hide his interest in Savannah. His emotion. He might be forgiven for thinking he should come to her rescue. She can be quite beguiling, but ultimately she's a liar. Always has been. A spoiled princess who ran away because she didn't get her way. Your boy isn't the first young man to fall under her spell."

Colton saw right through the man's little speech, but he also saw no percentage in either arguing or pretending to go along with it. This Laurencett character wouldn't let his guard down whether Colton pretended to be swayed by his lies or continued to protest his role in the rescue. Plan A was shot to hell. Time to improvise. Patiently.

"Why don't you just shut the hell up and get on with it?"

Laurencett's lips curled in a knowing smirk. "A man of action, eh? Well, you should know we already shut your boy down. Your rescue mission is over. The only thing left to determine is how Mama Sanci wants to deal with you and the governor."

Colton's heart pounded with the news that Trip had been taken. Shut down. What did that even mean? He had to trust they wouldn't have killed him. He hadn't heard any gunfire, though there had been that scuffle upstairs. Colton remained silent, waiting.

"You're a tough old nut, aren't you? Shame this didn't work out. You might have had a future as someone's security detail."

Colton just lifted a brow to convey his desire to get on with it without saying the words again.

"Very well. Nice and slow then. I'll have your sidearm. The one in the shoulder holster and the one in the ankle holster."

Colton began to reach for his .45, and Laurencett tutted. "Keep in mind, I don't have to be an expert marksman at this range. Two fingers please. I want to avoid the paperwork, if at all possible."

Doing what he was told, Colton slowly removed the revolver from his shoulder holster.

"On the floor," the agent said, and Colton eased into a crouch to set it down. Then he slipped the little P380 out of the ankle holster and set it beside the other weapon. "Back up."

Rising to take two long steps backwards, Colton watched as Laurencett kicked both weapons back into the bathroom and shut the door. Then he jerked the muzzle of his pistol down the hall toward the kitchen.

SAVANNAH STRUGGLED NOT to react as she followed Bethany onto the veranda to stand behind her mother. This put her in the perfect position to see when Trip—a scarlet silk pillow case over his head—was brought onto the porch and pushed to his knees in front of *Moman's* chair. Moments later Laurencett shoved Colton Jr. in, forcing him to his knees beside his son. Thankfully all attention was on the men, because she wasn't sure she managed to keep a neutral expression.

"What the hell is going on here?" Governor Krause asked, sitting forward in his chair.

"Explain yourself." *Moman's* voice, directed at Laurencett, brooked no delay and no deception.

"Seems there's more going on here than meets the eye," he said in answer. Savannah shuddered at the grim smile on his face. "These men are not here for the governor's security, are they, Savannah?"

She glanced at the governor. She could see the wheels turning in his mind as he tried to figure out what to say.

To her surprise, *Moman* sat back in her chair, stroking the arm of it thoughtfully.

"You surprise me, James," she said after a long moment of silence. "I thought you had come to be convinced into supporting my bid for governor. But this is something else, isn't it?"

Recognizing the tone in her mother's voice, Savannah braced herself. She didn't know what was going to happen, only that it wasn't going to be pleasant.

"I'm sure I don't know what you mean . . . ," Governor Krause began, but *Moman* cut him off with a wave of her hand.

"Of course you do," she snapped. "You're not stupid, and not so desperate for help you'd hire just any *dròl blofé* off the street to protect your person. Do you know how I know if *my* man is telling the truth?" She only paused for half a beat. "Because he knows how long liars last in my employ and what the consequences of *termination* are. So, when he says there's more you're not telling me, I trust him implicitly."

Governor Krause stood slowly, arms hanging loosely at his sides in the manner of a completely relaxed gentleman. Yet somehow he didn't look like someone who was ready to concede defeat, or to surrender.

"Very well," he said. "You tell me what you think is going on here."

In horror, Savannah watched as *Moman's* gaze moved from the governor to Colton Jr. to Trip, then swiveled around to look at her.

And her mother laughed. A short, sharp crack of sound that had no humor in it whatsoever.

"*Bondjé*! I taught you too well, child. Or not well enough. I cannot decide."

Savannah felt heat rush to her cheeks as her mother's words shamed her. She tried to maintain her composure, to not give away how clear her head was, but *Moman's* eyes narrowed before she turned back to the Thomas men.

"My child, she is a gifted actress, *non?* She even had me fooled. She wrapped you both around her little finger to get you here, to come to her aid. But do you know what is the most sad? You never had a hope of saving her, and now. . . now you will die because of her."

Savannah's gaze flew to the Thomas men, afraid what

they would think. She couldn't bear the thought of them believing she had only been using them. Except she had, at least at first.

If she hadn't been looking at Colton Jr., she would not have seen his hand creeping under the lapel of his jacket, toward a . . . . Was he reaching for a gun?

Her heart leapt into her throat, and she bit her lip in an attempt to not give him away. Something must have shown on her face because Laurencett stepped forward and raised his pistol.

chapter
twenty-six

S till blinded by the bag over his head, Trip had very little idea what was going on until Mama Sanci spoke. Even then he was still in the literal and figurative dark, but he knew where he was, and whose body had crashed against him moments before.

"Daddy?" he whispered.

"Son." It wasn't the encouragement he'd been hoping for.

He couldn't concentrate on the conversation around him. There had been some sound, or the scent of some perfume, that told him Savannah was nearby. All his focus went to trying to tell if she was okay. Until there was a sharp crack of sound—not a gunshot, but still frightening as to what it could mean—and his father fell against him with a grunt of pain.

"Daddy?" he said. As the body slid down against him on its way to the floor, a panicked noise came from his throat. For the first time, he truly struggled against the ties binding his hands behind his back, tried to shake the bag off his head, scrabbled his feet against the floor, tried to stand. For his efforts, he was pushed down, face first, to land across a body. His father's body. Through his panic, he could feel the rise and fall of his chest, which gave him some hope. Daddy was still alive.

Without warning the sack was pulled off, and Trip blinked in the sudden brightness of the veranda. A rough hand pulled his shoulder to flip him over, and he found himself staring up at Laurencett.

"Be glad you're tied up so you don't have the opportunity to attempt something foolish, as your father just did."

"Why not?" he said, his voice sounding like a growl to his own ears. "We're already as good as dead, aren't we?"

"Are you trying to make the case *for* killing you now? Boy, are you really that dumb? Don't answer that." Laurencett's gaze flicked to the right, and Trip saw Savannah standing behind her mother, a look of terror frozen on her face. "You will behave and do as you're told. That will determine what happens to the girl. Mama Sanci may allow her to live, if she doesn't decide she's a lost cause like you and your father."

"Surely you're not mad enough to do this in front of me," Governor Krause said. Trip noticed for the first time Jimmy was being restrained by two men in black suits. "Nothing done so far has been irredeemable. Let me get medical care for my man and we can call this a misunderstanding—an accident."

Laurencett only smiled. "Too bad the voters didn't ever learn about your decided lack of humor, sir." His mocking tone was crystal clear. "I, on the other hand, have a fine imagination. I'm certain I'll come up with a suitable story. It won't take long to convince them once I flash my badge around a bit."

Trip was frozen to the spot, unsure what to do. For all his talk of expecting to die, he wanted to live. He wanted Savannah to live. And Jesus knew he wanted his father to live. There had to be something, some way out of this mess, but he sure didn't see it.

Governor Krause was still talking, trying to make the FBI agent and Mama Sanci see reason, but Trip didn't think he was making any headway.

He met Savannah's gaze. Terror shone in her eyes, along with something else. He expected despair, maybe, but what he saw was more like determination. She was going to try something. Trip didn't know what, but he knew he needed to be ready for anything.

He wished he still had his ear bud so he could hear what Pitbull was up to. It was long gone, either dislodged in the struggle upstairs or removed while he had been knocked out. He wondered why the team hadn't already crashed through the front door to protect the governor. Surely they'd heard what was going on from the governor's own wire. Maybe they'd been neutralized. At this point it wouldn't surprise Trip to learn Mama Sanci had an army at her beck and call.

"Enough," Mama Sanci said, halting the battle of words between Jimmy and the FBI agent. "Deal with the details later. I am done with all this *boulvèrse*."

Several things happened at once. The governor took a step back, but was blocked from creating any real distance by the two muscular henchmen and a man in a classic butler's getup. The FBI agent raised his weapon and pointed it at the governor. Mama Sanci turned away, and Savannah . . . . Savannah lurched forward and fell at her mother's feet, the sheer robe swirling around her.

"*Moman*," she said, her voice breaking on the word. "Don't do this thing. I'd offer you my loyalty and my life, forever, but I don't think that will make any difference. You've gone too far." She reached out and took her mother's hands. Surprisingly, the woman did not resist. "All I can do is beg for your mercy. Please, *Moman*. Let us all live in peace."

As the woman's long, elegant fingers found and tightened on her daughter's hands, Trip thought for a second it was going to work, that Mama Sanci would capitulate to her daughter's request, but the woman's expression hardened.

"Why couldn't you show this desire to please me sooner, Savannah?" Mama Sanci said, sighing heavily. "It could have saved so much distress. Of course, these men might still have sought to rescue you. No, this is a sorry bed you have made. You must lie in it and suffer the guilt of knowing the fault is yours. For however much longer you shall live. Which, now that I think of it, shan't be long. After all, I was first elected after your father died. Will not the voters elect me again after seeing me grieve my daughter's death? Taken from us all too soon, and in such a violent manner as a home invasion."

Noting how the crazy woman's speech had caught everyone's attention, including the FBI agent's, Trip glanced at his father, who made a motion like throwing a lasso. Trip instantly knew what he meant and made his move—the only move he could make.

Falling to his side, he rolled over and, with the skill borne of roping many a fractious calf, knocked the agent's feet out from under him, then brought his still-bound arms around the man's neck, putting him into a stranglehold.

He was aware of his father in motion, though he didn't know what his target was.

The agent's pistol—Trip hoped it was the only weapon in the room—flew several feet to land on the floor between Savannah and her mother. The two women looked at the weapon, then at each other, then both lunged for it, ending up grappling.

Laurencett was still struggling against his chokehold. For a moment, all Trip's attention was taken in holding onto the man. When he peered back up, the veranda seemed filled with more people than had been there moments before.

A shot rang out, and everyone stilled as a single figure slumped to the floor.

SAVANNAH NEARLY DROPPED the gun when she felt the recoil of the shot, but she and her mother locked gazes, and she saw something like madness in the woman's eyes. In desperation, she wrenched the weapon away, knocking her mother to the floor in the process. Only then did she risk a look to see what was going on in the rest of the room.

Trip held a struggling Laurencett in a chokehold on the floor. The governor was in a fistfight with two men. Colton Jr. was down again, a blossom of red marring the white of his linen suit.

"*Bondjé!*" she whispered, realizing he'd been shot by the gun she was holding.

Before she could process the idea that she may have just killed a man—a friend, the father of the man she loved —a commotion erupted from the front of the house. Seconds after that, more shouting came from the backyard and a dozen men in white suits came charging out of the house, around the columns, and up onto the veranda.

Savannah's response was immediate: she threw up her hands and backed away from her mother before dropping to her knees. The butler did the same, and the other men stopped fighting as the shouting men in uniforms bore down on them.

Trip, his father, and the governor stood still, hands out in the open and away from any area someone might assume could conceal a gun.

Moman, recovered from the shock of the pistol's discharge, appeared to be looking for just the right thing to say to mitigate the damage of being caught in. . . whatever the press would make out of this mess.

In mere moments, each man who had been struggling for their lives had automatic rifles aimed at their hearts, and the veranda was steeped in sudden silence, broken only by Colton Jr.'s labored breathing.

The notable exception was Governor James.

"Sir?" one of the armed men gave the governor a side-eye look, not taking his focus from one of *Moman's* body-guards who stood before him.

"Impeccable timing, son." Jimmy glanced at Colton Jr.'s blood-stained jacket. "Well. . . nearly. This man needs to get to the hospital immediately. See to it."

One of the men on the edge of the veranda broke away, hand up to key the throat mic of his tactical radio.

Savannah turned her attention to her mother, unsure what was going to happen next. *Moman* didn't look like someone whose plans had just been shattered. Didn't even look like a kid caught with her hand in the cookie jar.

Moman visibly drew herself up to her full height and addressed the man who had spoken to the governor.

"How dare you burst in here like you think you're making a 'drug bust,'" she spat, making air quotes. "This is a private residence. The mayor's private residence. I don't know what you think is happening, but I'll see to it you lose your job for interfering."

The man didn't bother to respond, and the governor gave a derisive snort.

"Nice try, Madame Mayor, but these men don't answer to you."

Moman snarled at him, and for a long moment Savannah thought she might actually try to strike. But the moment passed, and *Moman* seemed to deflate when no one budged an inch toward bending to her will.

Governor Krause stepped slowly toward Savannah and held out a hand. It wasn't until that moment she remembered she was still holding the gun. She handed it to him, grip first, and he took it, engaged the safety, then held it out for one of his men to collect.

Then he smiled gently and offered her a hand up.

She took it, rising unsteadily to her feet, and he turned to the lead officer. "This little lady and the two fellas in white are with me. Everyone else can be taken into custody."

"On what charges?" *Moman* protested.

"Kidnapping, for starters," he began.

"But she's my daughter!"

"She's been drugged and brought here against her will. We might even add trafficking to the list, the way you were pushing her at me. And before you protest again that she's your daughter, remember it's a sad fact that people traffic their own children all the time. What else?"

"Aggravated assault," Colton Jr. offered from where he sat on the wicker loveseat, applying pressure to the bullet hole in his shoulder.

"Attempted murder," Trip added, getting into the spirit of things. "And that would be two counts of kidnapping, given how I was tied up and moved against my will."

Jimmy nodded. "And I'm sure if we look close enough, we'll find plenty of other. . . shady practices that won't hold up to the light of day. Like bribing an elected official, not to mention an officer of the law. Yes ma'am, I'd say you're in a heap of trouble."

Savannah didn't truly relax until her mother and Albert had cuffs on them and were being led away, a surly Laurencett bundled off behind them.

Not long after that the ambulance arrived, and the EMTs began to work on Trip's father.

"How are you?" Trip's voice, so close to her ear, made her jump. "Sorry. I didn't mean to startle you."

She put a hand to her chest in an effort to calm her racing heart. "I don't know," she told him truthfully. "I'm so sorry about your father. I never meant to let anyone get hurt."

"It might be a good idea to get you checked out at the hospital too," the governor said, walking up. "That's his daddy getting loaded up now. Why don't you all ride to the hospital with Junior? They've been pumping you up with some kind of sedative for quite some time, and that can have some bad effects."

Trip nodded.

"You're going too?" she asked, clutching at his arm.

"Of course he is," the governor insisted.

"Won't we have to make statements or something?" Trip asked. "I mean, I don't want these. . . these people to get off on a technicality . . . ."

"Not likely, son," the governor said. "I still had my earpiece in, and Pitbull recorded everything from the support vehicle. Not to mention my reputation as a Louisiana's only lonely honest politician. No, we'll get your statements at the hospital. Don't you worry about it."

In a different kind of daze, Savannah let Trip guide her to the ambulance, where he helped her inside and then climbed up beside her. It was a tight fit with the two of them, the gurney with Colton Jr., and the EMT who was watching his vitals while they rolled through the streets toward the nearest hospital.

Savannah leaned against Trip, one hand wrapped around his firm forearm while he pulled her against him.

"You came." Getting her voice above a whisper proved impossible. Trip leaned down to hear her better. She cleared her throat and tried again. "You came for me."

"Of course I did," he said, voice as soft as her own. "I said I'd protect you, didn't I?"

chapter
twenty-seven

I t was over. That thought echoed in Trip's mind as he held Savannah close and listened to her cry softly against his chest. Her tears were heartbreaking, and he didn't know what to do or say to comfort her. Wasn't exactly sure why she was crying.

Yes, they'd managed to rescue her, but her mother was on her way to jail, she'd seen a man shot by the weapon she'd been holding, and she'd been drugged out of her mind for at least twenty-four hours, if not longer. He didn't dare hope any of her tears were of joy at him being there with her. But he wanted that—wanted her to share his joy at their reunion.

He just hoped it would mean to her what it meant to him. And while he wanted nothing more than to kiss her 'til she was senseless, he knew he needed to take his time with her.

Savannah had been through a lot. He could wait until she got her life, or at least her emotions, back in order.

"You'll be okay," he said for the tenth time, as much to reassure himself as her.

Her fingers tightened around his forearm in response and she nodded, her tears finally beginning to slow.

He let his gaze drift to his father again, and tried not to worry about his drawn, pale features. There had been a lot of blood, and he knew his father well enough to know when the man was putting on a brave face.

This was no bump on the head or even a broken bone. This was a bullet wound that could have done a great deal of damage. Only a doctor and an x-ray could tell how much.

Given the time of evening, the ambulance made good speed to the hospital. Once they came to a stop near the entrance to the emergency department, Trip handed Savannah down into the helpful arms of the driver. He climbed out himself and turned to watch as they unloaded his father.

The gurney jerked as the wheels dropped to the ground, and his father winced before his stoic expression returned. A doctor met them at the door and began quizzing the EMTs for information. The words came in snatches, most of which meant little to Trip.

"GSW to the shoulder . . . . BP falling . . . . Lucid, but in pain . . . . Compression only to the wound . . . ."

Trip stopped trying to understand their verbal short-hand, focusing instead on his father as he trotted alongside the gurney.

There was a point at last where an attendant in scrubs snagged his sleeve, telling him he couldn't go any farther. Even family wasn't allowed into the OR.

The OR. Operating room. His father was going to be operated on. He stood in the hallway, staring past the large double doors his father had vanished through.

He was going to have to tell his mother.

It wasn't until long moments later he realized he'd lost track of Savannah.

SAVANNAH WATCHED Trip follow the doctors as they wheeled Colton Jr. away before finally turning her attention to the nurse waiting impatiently beside her.

"*Mo chagrin*," she said. "I'm sorry. What?"

The nurse sighed and repeated himself. "Are you injured?"

"I . . . ." Her mind didn't want to focus. The adrenaline that had kept her sharp during the struggle was gone, wept out with the tears she'd cried on Trip's shoulder. Now there was only unbearable exhaustion.

"I . . . ." she tried again, her legs wobbling. She reached out a hand to steady herself against the nurse but missed.

Her last thought was, *I can't faint. Not now*, as she began to topple over, darkness crashing across her vision in a swift wave.

INDISTINCT VOICES BEGAN to clarify as Savannah's eyelids fluttered. Recognizing the same surroundings, she thought she must not have been out very long, but a different face was hovering in front of her.

She was on the floor, she realized, then a bright light flashed in her eyes.

"Her pupils are blown. Is she high? Look at the way she's dressed. Is she a working girl?"

She wanted to sit up but couldn't make her arms work. "Not high," she tried to say. "Drugged."

"What'd she say?"

"I think she said she's been drugged."

"Where'd she come from?"

"Not sure. Ambulance brought in a GSW, then she was standing here."

The woman in the white coat helped her sit up. "Can you tell us your name?"

Savannah nodded but couldn't make her mouth work.

The doctor turned to the nurse. "Is that Jay's unit? Find him and see what he knows."

When the nurse left, the doctor returned her attention to Savannah. "I'm Doctor Liz Pettitclaire. Can you tell me your name?"

"I . . . ." she started, then stopped, remembering she could give her real name. "Savannah. Savannah Montault de Saint-Cirié."

"Very good," the doctor said. If she recognized the name, she didn't let it show. "And do you know what happened to you?"

"Someone gave me something. To make me do what they wanted me to do." She struggled to say the words in English and not slip into Creole.

The doctor didn't even blink. "Was it a pill? Mixed in a drink?"

Savannah shook her head, and the doctor's eyes widened. "Injection, I think. And in a drink."

There were more questions Savannah tried to answer as best as she could before a wheelchair was brought and she was helped to sit.

Someone—she thought it was the ambulance driver— arrived, and a hushed conversation ensued. Then the doctor crouched beside the chair, facing her.

"We're going to get you fixed right up," she said. Savannah nodded, though her gaze had been drawn to Trip, who stood across the room, eyes scanning the room restlessly until he saw her.

Relief flooded through her as he headed toward her, and she felt warmth returning, telling her how cold she'd been until that moment.

"This isn't the man who . . . ?" the doctor began. Savannah shook her head.

"This is the man who saved me."

TRIP WAS dead on his feet. There had been non-stop activity since their arrival at the hospital several hours ago, broken only by short breaks between interviews with detectives and agents and one very sly reporter who'd managed to sneak in to ask, "In your own words, tell me what happened?"

It had taken longer than he cared to admit to catch on to the man's duplicity.

There had also been a couple updates from the surgeon on Daddy's condition.

The initial bullet retrieval had gone well, but there was damage to the bones in his shoulder, still too early to tell how extensive. A specialist had taken over and was still working.

Savannah was another concern. They'd been separated for the interviews while she was in a fragile state. All Trip could do was hope the authorities would take that into consideration.

At the moment, he sat on the edge of a chair in the waiting room, elbows on knees, hands still clasped from the last prayer he'd sent up to heaven, head hanging in utter weariness.

Something, some sense of being watched, made him look up, and he saw Savannah standing not far from him. She looked pale and just as tired as he felt, but stronger than she'd seemed before. Someone had given her hospital scrubs to cover the skimpy nightgown she'd arrived in, but she still looked beautiful to him.

He stood and hesitantly opened his arms, unsure after all this how she truly felt about him.

To his immense relief, she snaked her arms around his waist as he enfolded her in a gentle hug. With her cheek against his chest, he could tell she was speaking, but he couldn't make out her words.

"I'm sorry, love. What was that?"

She tilted her head to look up at him, and when she spoke, he heard her plainly.

"Never since my *popa* died have I felt so safe and loved. You not only came all the way out here to find me but risked your life to save me. I understand the governor was in on your plan, and that's good, but *Moman* . . . . If you hadn't come, there's no telling what she would have used me for. I'm more grateful to you than I can ever say."

Trip squeezed her close, at a loss for words. How could he tell her what had motivated him? She seemed to think he'd come out of some noble sense of duty. The reality was much simpler than that, yet so much more complicated.

"How could I not come?" he said at last. "I love you." He waited, tense, for her reaction. If she even had a reaction. She'd been through so much . . . .

When she took a moment before pulling back, he feared the worst. The tears shining in her eyes did not reassure him.

"Oh Trip," she said at last. "What did I ever do to deserve a champion like you?"

She stood on tiptoe to kiss him. It was not a deeply sensual kiss like their first, but neither was it a chaste peck on the cheek like a woman would give a pathetic loser.

"I hope you won't regret your love for such an unworthy woman," she said, "or come to hate me when time shows you just how unworthy I am."

"That's your mother talking," he said firmly, taking her face in his hands to make her look at him. "I reckon time will prove you were more like yourself when you were out at the Lazy J than you ever could be here. And I'm pretty dang patient when I need to be. I'll wait. That is, if you'll let me."

The smile she gave him was tremulous but sweet, completely disarming him. He wanted to sweep her off her feet and carry her to safety, as absurd as that would be given he was a thousand miles from the only safe place he could think of.

"I think—no, I'd love it if you show me."

Her words were almost shy, but he thought he detected a hint of that mischievous sparkle he loved so much. Letting a slow smile curve his lips upward, he lowered his head to kiss her forehead, then her nose, then her lips . . . . Again, not much more than the lightest touch, but with it he tried to convey a promise. A promise he would not only show her what he saw in her to love, but love and protect her for as long as she would let him.

When he pulled away, her eyes shone up at him, holding a similar promise.

chapter
twenty-eight

A s much as Trip wanted to leave New Orleans, his departure was not in the cards for at least a week, maybe more.

With Daddy in the hospital, the first thing he had to do after the police were done with him was to call Momma, and of course she was going to fly down immediately.

Daddy had been in surgery for over four hours, between the initial retrieval of the bullet and the specialist who had to reconstruct the collar bone the bullet had shattered. By the time he called Momma they had closed him up, but he still hadn't awakened. For a few moments Trip had thought Blue and Janie were going to insist on coming, but he was able to assure them the doctor was confident Daddy was out of danger.

The early morning call—even earlier for the family at the Lazy J—had been the hardest he'd ever had to make. A hundred times harder than the call he'd made after wrecking Daddy's pickup when he was only fifteen.

As he ended the call, he felt a weariness deep in his soul, and realized it had been. . . what? Seventy-two hours since he'd had any decent sleep? The police had released him for the time being but told him he should remain in town until further notice in case they needed more information. As if he would go anywhere while his father was still in the hospital.

Savannah had clung to his side as much as he clung to her. Now, as he looked down to see she had fallen asleep with her cheek against his chest, he wondered what to do.

Eventually he thought of the hotel where he and Daddy had left their things. It was as good a place as any. Savannah couldn't go home even if she'd wanted to, what with it being a crime scene and all.

Using his phone one-handed, he figured out how to search for a taxi service and managed to arrange a pickup without waking Savannah.

When the nurse at the desk by the waiting room door asked who was expecting a cab, Trip gathered Savannah in his arms and carried her out into the pre-dawn light. She barely stirred as he settled her into the cab and didn't wake at all when they arrived at the hotel.

The driver, a kindly black man with a heavy accent not unlike Savannah's, unlocked the room door so Trip could carry her inside. It turned out he had heard about the event on the morning news, and Trip had to force the man to take his money.

"That woman," the driver said, "some of us know about her true self. She called us 'darkies' and 'niggas' as if she ain't got none of our blood in her body. When I heard she was running for governor, I prayed she would be exposed for the hateful woman she is. My cousin, you see, she worked for the mayor and told us how she wasn't getting paid enough to be treated worse than a mangy cat in the street. She also told us about poor miss there, and how she was expected to do shameful things she clearly didn't want to do. If you had anything to do with bringing that evil woman down, I bless you."

In the end, Trip had to slip the fare into the man's breast pocket and hold it there for a moment until the man nodded at last and returned to his cab.

As he closed the door and turned to see Savannah where the cabbie had helped him tuck her beneath the covers, his only thoughts were of sleep.

He lay down atop the covers beside her, placing one hand gently on her hip, and closed his eyes. Sleep claimed him instantly.

SAVANNAH WOKE SLOWLY and tensed when she realized she wasn't alone. Someone was beside her, snoring softly. Something heavy weighted the covers on one side, making her feel half-trapped. Even so, it was several moments before she opened her eyes.

The room was dim, but she could tell it was daylight outside. She could make out furniture—unfamiliar furniture—the closest being another bed next to where she lay. Made up and smooth, unoccupied.

A hotel, she realized.

She turned her head, struggling to remember how she'd arrived in this place and terrified at the thought of who she would find beside her.

At the sight of Trip's face, relaxed in a deep sleep, all the tension drained out of her. She still didn't remember much, but if Trip were here, she was safe.

The call of nature—what had woken her in the first place—returned. As gently as she could, she extricated herself from the covers and made her way into the tiny bathroom.

Once relieved, she took a moment to pull back the curtain enough to look out the window. It was evening, clouds lit up fiery red by the setting sun. Several folks sat on the patio furniture, apparently enjoying the cooling weather. They looked to be laughing, but the hum of the room's air conditioner drowned out any noise from outside.

The longer she was awake, the more she remembered what had happened—thankfully in reverse order so she never lost the knowledge that she was safe.

Safe in the company of a man who loved her.

That thought alone should have given her pause. After all, he had fallen for a woman who had been playing a part, doing what she had to do to survive.

She'd lied to him and his family, told them what she thought they needed to hear so they would take her in. But it hadn't all been lies, had it?

Yes, she had given them a false history, but had she really been acting while she lived and worked at the Lazy J? Cooking was her passion. It had been all her life. And she'd found a true sense of pride and pleasure in serving the ranch hands.

When she held that up against what Trip had said earlier, that she'd been her true self when she'd been on the ranch, she couldn't really disagree.

Maybe he had a point. Maybe the woman he loved really was her, not just some fiction she had invented in order to survive.

Standing there looking down at the cowboy who had come to her rescue, she touched her lips, remembering his sweet kiss, and wondered if there was any chance for them.

As she pondered what the future might hold, he

opened one eye and looked up at her, a lazy smile coming to his lips for one sweet moment. Then he opened his other eye, his smile giving way to concern as he woke fully to the reality of where they were and why.

"What time is it?" He shifted onto his back and pulled at the pillow until it supported him in a more upright position.

She glanced at the clock on the table on the other side of the second bed.

"Six. Just don't ask me what day it is."

He gave a rueful smile and patted the bed beside him. She sat, stiffly for a moment, but it wasn't long before she gave in to her longing and lay down beside him, curling into him and spreading her left hand on his chest.

"I reckon it's still Wednesday. Momma said she was coming right away. Even if she's flying commercial, I reckon it won't be much more than twenty-four hours before she gets here. And I told her to call me in time to meet her at the hospital."

"You sure you didn't miss any calls?" she murmured.

He chuckled. "No, I'm not. Can't say I'm even sure where my phone is."

She felt him patting the bed beside him, then shifting as he checked the back pocket that didn't exist in the suit pants he still wore.

"I should let you up to find it," she said, though she didn't move to do so.

"Yes, you should," he agreed, but he put a hand over hers and squeezed, letting her know he wasn't in a hurry to move. "Eventually," he finished.

His chest rose and fell as he heaved a sigh. "I hope it's all right that I brought you here. I didn't know where else to go."

"There's nowhere I'd rather be."

He squeezed her hand again, but didn't say anything else. What else was there to say?

She listened to his heart beating beneath her ear and gloried in the moment, knowing she was safe. . . and loved.

She must have fallen asleep again. The next thing she knew Trip was shifting beneath her, reaching for a ringing phone. She rolled onto her back and stretched her arms over her head as he picked up the room's old-fashioned handset.

"Hello?" His voice was thick with sleep. "Yes, of course. Thank you." There was a pause, then, "I'm sorry, Momma. The battery must have died." Another pause. Savannah could hear a voice on the line, but she couldn't make out any words. "All right. I'll be there as soon as I can. I love you too."

The handset clattered as he hung it up on the base unit. She looked over at him as the bed shifted. He was sitting on the edge of the mattress, rubbing his eyes.

"She's at the hospital," he said. "Good thing I remembered to tell them where we were staying. I guess my phone is dead."

"Your father?" she asked.

"Not awake yet. They said that's normal enough after such extensive surgery. Momma only just arrived from the airport. She tried to make out like she's fine, but I can tell she wants to see me, to be sure I'm still whole."

"Of course," Savannah said, suddenly unsure what she should be doing.

"I'm going to take a quick shower and change." He turned to look at her. "You don't have any fresh clothes . . . ."

"You want me to come with you?" she asked in surprise.

"I was hoping . . . . That is, if you want to . . . ."

All she could do was nod. She'd meant what she'd said before, about not knowing anywhere else she'd rather be. Only. . . it wasn't any place, it was him. Wherever he was, that was where she wanted to be.

"It'll be. . . I mean, won't it feel like a walk of shame if you come along wearing the same clothes?"

She smiled. "Perhaps you have a shirt I can wear?"

In the end, she pulled one of his father's shirts over the chemise top she'd worn since the night her mother had offered her to Governor Krause. Someone at the hospital had given her scrubs to wear, and she had no other pants to wear now, but just taking a quick shower—Trip insisted she go before him—and slipping the clean shirt on made her feel at least a little fresher. Her hair was a mass of tangles she couldn't even work her fingers through, but it stayed in a knot at the back of her neck when she twisted and tied it back. It would have to do until she had time to get something that would tame it.

Trip came out of the shower wrapped only in a towel and stopped short when he saw her. They stared at each other for a long moment before he walked to where she sat on the edge of the bed.

She felt the heat rising in her cheeks—and indeed her whole body—as he stopped two feet in front of her. His left hand secured the towel at his hip, but he lifted his free right hand and touched her cheek. She raised her gaze to meet his eyes.

She'd only been looking at his hands, she told herself. His strong, capable hands . . . .

He inhaled deeply, then let the breath out slowly.

"I'd love to explore what that look on your face means, Miss Savannah," he said at last, "but when I do, we're going to have time to enjoy ourselves."

She shivered lightly at the promise in those words. "I

look forward to that day," she said in a low voice, smiling up at him.

They held hands in the cab on the ride over to the hospital but didn't speak much beyond a comment on the changing weather—it was raining in earnest now—and when the driver pulled up under the covered main entrance, they had a brief exchange.

She waited, feeling ever more out of place, while Trip —dressed now in familiar denim—checked in at the first nurse's station they came to. His father was in the ICU, recently moved there from recovery. That was a good sign, wasn't it? She wasn't well-versed in the sequence of healing from a gunshot wound.

Eventually they were directed to the right room, and Savannah was allowed to accompany Trip after he insisted she was family too—a sentiment that touched her deeply.

Maddy rushed to engulf her son in a fierce hug, pulling back only for a moment when she reached out to include Savannah.

She whispered something to Trip and hugged them both so tightly, Savannah thought she heard bones creaking under the pressure. When at last she loosened her hold, they all turned as one to look at the figure lying on the bed.

The man was so pale and drawn, Savannah almost couldn't recognize Trip's father. She put a hand up to her mouth to hold back a sound of dismay.

"*Bondjé!*" she whispered. "*Mo chagrin.* This is down to me, Maddy. I am so sorry!"

Maddy didn't loosen her grip on Savannah's shoulders. "Oh sweetheart. Trip told me what happened. There's no way you're to blame for this."

"But I was holding the gun when it went off. It was my struggle with *Moman* that made this happen."

"The way I heard it, there would have been a lot more shooting—or worse—if you hadn't stepped in at that moment. If you're up for it, why don't you both tell me everything? I want to know how this all went down."

SAVANNAH WASN'T sure how long it took for them to tell Maddy the whole story. She and Trip alternated, each filling in gaps the other didn't know, until they got caught up to meeting Maddy in Colton's room at the hospital.

She was repeatedly gratified by the lengths the men had gone to in their efforts to rescue her. The idea that she was worthy of such dogged determination. . . it almost defied belief.

But there she was, safe, being told all that had happened was not her fault—another truth she found hard to accept, no matter how often they repeated the words.

Trip's growling stomach broke the quiet that had fallen over the room, causing the three of them to chuckle.

"I'll see if I can't rustle up some grub," Trip said, rising from the chair he'd positioned at the foot of Colton's bed. She and Maddy shared the wide bench seat at the window overlooking the lights of the city. "It's late, but there's bound to be a vending machine if the cafeteria is closed."

Silence held for long moments after he left, until Maddy heaved a sigh.

"Lord, but this brings back bittersweet memories," she said, gazing at her husband with a loving vulnerability that evoked both pity and a bit of jealousy in Savannah.

"He's been hurt before?"

Maddy chuckled. "He's been hurt many times, but

mostly just the kinds of accidents that happen on a ranch. This isn't the first time he's been shot, though."

"It sounds like there's a story in there somewhere," she said, seeing an opportunity to learn more about this man who risked his life for her.

"Yes indeed. All the elements of a romance for the ages. You might not know it to look at me now, but I once had two men chasing after my affection. Colton and his older brother, Blue. I was sweet on Blue, but too selfish to tell them I'd made my choice between them. I liked the attention, I'm afraid. And then the draft came and took them both away from me. Well, the draft took Blue, and Colton just plain lied about his age so he could volunteer and serve with his brother. He's always had that drive to protect his loved ones."

She stood and moved to the bedside, taking her husband's hand. "Only Colton came back."

After a long, long moment, she continued. "We had our share of drama after that. First with his recovery—he'd been shot up pretty badly—then as he battled PTSD while a rival tried to take the ranch . . . . He was so wound up, he almost let me slip through his fingers."

"It's a good thing for me you're such a stubborn woman," a groggy voice broke in. They both turned to see Colton looking up at them with eyes open, a slightly loopy grin lifting the corners of his mouth.

It was such a welcome sight, Savannah once again clapped her hand over her mouth, then looked away as Maddy stooped to kiss the man she loved.

epilogue

Savannah held herself a little apart from the group of Thomas family folks gathered around Mitzi and little baby Bluebelle.

Even after six months she still felt overwhelmed by this family. Not that they were hard to be around. On the contrary, they were kind and loveable and had welcomed her as though she'd been in the family her whole life.

And that was the idea that overwhelmed her. Since her *popa* died, she'd become accustomed to being more of an asset than a daughter—something to be used as needed and kept out of sight, out of mind in between. But the Thomas family . . . .

Not only did they engage her services as a cook and laundress, they included her in family functions and family discussions on a daily basis.

Of course, it didn't hurt that Trip was completely in love with her—a feeling she fully requited—but she felt they would treat her the same anyway.

As if sensing her thoughts, Trip found her gaze and crooked a finger to encourage her to join them. Smiling, she closed the distance between them, and Trip curled his arm around her waist to give her a squeeze while the others conversed.

Mitzi laughed and punched her husband's arm. "We were *not* going to name her Periwinkle," she explained for the group. "That was just Blue's threat to get me to agree to Bluebelle. I wanted to call her Carrie May."

"Which is how we landed on Bluebelle May," Blue said. "Compromise."

Trip snorted at what was surely the understatement of the century. Maddy, who was holding the baby, turned to chastise him and instead caught sight of Savannah. She held Bluebelle out and said, "Do you want to hold her?"

The thought terrified her. To be given that tiny life to hold mere hours after her birth . . . .

But Maddy's smile was gentle and full of confidence in her, so Savannah reached out.

The baby was both lighter and heavier than she'd expected—like picking up an object that didn't weigh as much as it looked, but oh, the heaviness of holding something so precious—and when she looked down, she had to admit to the cuteness of the little hands bunched into fists, held close to her chest like a prize fighter entering a boxing ring.

Then she opened her eyes, and Savannah lost herself in the soft, unfocused blue of that gaze. Trip, looking over her shoulder, tightened his arm around her waist, and Savannah thought about what Kate had done, and how this might have been hard on him—especially because so few people knew about it.

She looked up at him and smiled. "She's *adorabl*," she said, searching his gaze.

"Yeah," he agreed, his voice soft. "All the same, I'm not in an especial hurry for one of my own. There are a few things I gotta do first." She noticed a twinkle in his eye.

"Gotta find the right woman and convince her to marry me."

"Oh, well good luck with that," she said with an answering smile. "Seems like there ought to be someone around here willing to get saddled with you."

He pulled her even closer, ostensibly to get a better look at the baby, but he was only looking at her.

"You remember that first time I brought you a shot of hooch and we drank it on your porch? You asked me if there wasn't something in the air around here that made folks fall in love."

"I remember," she said, though she was surprised he did.

"Did you hear Janie proposed to Tim the other day? She got tired of waiting for him to believe she really didn't care about his history. They haven't set a date or anything, but he said yes."

That made Savannah smile. So very like Janie to take matters into her own hands.

"And you know how we all had our fifteen minutes of fame around the trial?"

That made Savannah grimace with distaste. Her mother's trial had come accompanied by a media circus and political nightmare.

Because the story that broke around her arrest was so close to the election, Mama Sanci lost her bid to be governor, as well as any credibility as a trustworthy politician. She'd initially denied any wrongdoing, but her time as mayor was still being investigated by FBI Headquarters. Everything else about her life fell under the media's microscope and she was vilified in the court of public opinion. She eventually waived an extended court battle in favor of a deal, the details of which were being kept under wraps.

Savannah still had nightmares about her mother getting out of jail and coming after her.

Bluebelle started to fuss as she transmitted her disquiet to the child, and Grandpa Colton held out a free hand for her. They'd all gotten a kick at how comfortable the nook between his chest and sling was for the baby.

"I remember," she said again, once all attention had fully followed Bluebelle.

"Well, Kylie's story came out, how she'd hoped to become a famous singer but was kidnapped instead."

Savannah nodded again. Just hearing that story had raised goosebumps on her arms.

"Turns out the interviewer 'knows a guy,' so she's got an interview. . . uh, audition, with a true studio rep. She and Jax are headed for Nashville in a couple weeks. You know, after we all get a chance to check that these guys are who they say they are."

"That's wonderful."

"I thought so too. And now little Belle is here on the scene, completing Blue's family. Only one to go."

She looked up at Trip, the love he felt for her shining in his eyes. "You mean somebody else still has to fall in love?"

"Nah. He just has to make it official."

Her heart rate sped up, pulsing in her chest. "How is he going to do that?"

"Well, if he was into dramatic romantic gestures, he'd drop to one knee in front of everyone and ask her to marry him, but honestly, he's kind of a fraidy-cat and worries what he'd do if she turned him down.

"Another option would be to take her out on a ride and tell some goofy story before making a heartfelt proposal, but it turns out his brother already did that."

"Oh," she said faintly, not sure what she thought of all

this talk about proposals. They weren't there yet. . . were they?

"But," he went on, "even though they've been through so much together, he realized that was the same reason he shouldn't rush into anything. I mean, he totally loves her and would happily spend the rest of his life just loving her, but is six months really enough time to know for sure? What do you think?"

As he gazed into her eyes with a steady and serious expression, she thought about what he was asking. Was six months long enough to know, *really know*, if someone was *the* someone, the one to spend the rest of their lives together?

But then she knew. She'd known it since she first met his gaze at that fundraiser in New Orleans. If not sooner. A girl could hardly do better than saying yes to Colton Thomas the Third.

"I think she'd be a fool to make him wait too long. She'd only be cheating herself out of more time with the best man she knows."

His eyes lit up. "Well then, at the risk of being accused of stealing Belle's thunder . . . ." He dropped to one knee in front of Savannah.

author's note

Louisiana Creole is considered an Endangered Language as fewer than 10,000 people in the world speak it. As such, it was difficult to find the words I needed. I tried to be faithful, but there *may* be a little Haitian Creole in one or two of the admittedly limited words and phrases I used, as that is one Creole language Google can translate. The words are similar to French and Cajun, but Louisiana Creole has unique spelling that looks more phonetic than its parent language. I hope you enjoyed reading about a language few folks speak, and want to learn more about it.

Yes, there is a story to tell about Maddy and Colton. It may also interest you to know I'm kicking around an idea for a story about the Original True Blue Thomas and how the Lazy J was founded. Real old school cowboy western stuff, with my stamp of suspenseful romance. Not sure when I'll get to tell them, but if I hear enough people are interested, that could put them on the front burner. So if you're interested, look me up on social media and let me know.

While I've got your attention, I'd like to acknowledge a few folks who helped me get this book to readers despite my workaday world's efforts to keep it under wraps. First, my alpha readers: Andie Lopata, who as a local let me know whether my depiction of all things New Orleans would fly; and my author friend Marissa Honeycutt, who delighted in reading something (a lot) lighter than her own works. This was a tricky one, and their observations helped tremendously. Thanks to Word Nerd Monica Black, who managed to edit Last Refuge for me while COVID worked its way through her whole family. 100covers.com made the beautiful cover for me. And more thanks to Marissa for formatting this and reformatting all my books. They're beautiful! And I can't neglect to mention my hubby, who proposed to me after only six months, and we're still going strong after nineteen years. Here's to (at least) 19 more, my honey.

Please consider leaving a review.

I love writing stories for you.

One of the best and most important ways *you* can help me continue to write them is to tell other people whether and how much you enjoy reading my work.

Reviews encourage other readers to try an author or a book they might not otherwise take a chance on. It helps an author on so many levels, and we're grateful when readers share their experience with a book.

So, don't be shy. Let the world know how you feel.

Post a dissertation. Post a paragraph. Post a sentence.

Or just post a star rating.

From an author's perspective, the only ineffective way to review is to not leave one at all.

Please consider posting your review with the vendor you purchased it from, and/or anywhere you visit to find the books you enjoy.

www.kristicramerbooks.com

*Visit **WattPad** for opening chapters of published works and sneak peeks at works in progress:* http://kcbooks.us/wpKCpro

the thomas family novels

Last Shot at Justice (#1)

Detective Mitzi Reardon just became the prime suspect in a murder she didn't commit. On the run from enemies and coworkers alike, Mitzi must put her trust in Blue Thomas, an old-school cowboy from Kansas.

Last Second Chance (#2)

Ex-con Tim Reardon finds more than his last chance at redemption at the Lazy J; he finds friendship, a purpose, and maybe even love. But his past is just on the horizon, waiting for a chance to swallow him up.

One Last Song (#3)

Kidnapped, Jax Belamy and Kylie Thomas must escape their captors before they're taken across the border into a human-trafficking nightmare.

Last Refuge (#4)

When the Lazy J Ranch finds itself in need of a cook, the arrival of a beautiful Creole woman seems to be a surprising answer to their prayers. Trip finds himself drawn to the mysterious woman, but there's far more to Savannah's story than she's letting on.

all titles by kristi cramer

In The Knights of Juneau (Adult Romantic Suspense)

Standalone novels featuring the Knight family, residents of Juneau, Alaska.

    Knight Before Dawn (#1)

The Thomas Family Novels (Suspense with a Dash of Romance)

Standalone novels featuring characters connected to the Thomas Family of Syracuse, Kansas.

    Last Shot at Justice (#1)

    Last Second Chance (#2)

    One Last Song (#3)

    Last Refuge (#4)

With Elaine Cramer (Adult Dark Humor)

A Sci-Fi short

    The Musician & the Alien

In the Magic of Verridian Series

Fantasy for the Whole Family

    To Make a King (#1)

Time Travel Adventures for the Whole Family

In the Fickle Universe

Sherwood Rogue

Find these (and other titles) at
www.kristicramerbooks.com